EXPECTING HIS LOVE-CHILD

BY
CAROL MARINELLI

™ MILLS & BOON®
Pure reading pleasure

All the characters in this book have no existence outside the imagination of the author, and have no relation whatsoever to anyone bearing the same name or names. They are not even distantly inspired by any individual known or unknown to the author, and all the incidents are pure invention.

First published in Great Britain 2007
Harlequin Mills & Boon Limited,
Eton House, 18-24 Paradise Road, Richmond, Surrey TW9 1SR

© Carol Marinelli 2007

ISBN: 978 0 263 86397 0

Set in Times Roman 10½ on 12¼ pt
01-0108-45895

Printed and bound in Spain
by Litografia Rosés, S.A., Barcelona

Carol Marinelli recently filled in a form where she was asked for her job title and was thrilled, after all these years, to be able to put down her answer as writer. Then it asked what Carol did for relaxation, and after chewing her pen for a moment Carol put down the truth—writing. The third question asked—what are your hobbies? Well, not wanting to look obsessed or, worse still, boring, she crossed the fingers on her free hand and answered swimming and tennis. But, given that the chlorine in the pool does terrible things to her highlights, and the closest she's got to a tennis racket in the last couple of years is watching the Australian Open—I'm sure you can guess the real answer!

Carol also writes for Medical™ Romance
Look out for another
HOUSE OF KOLOVSKY
story, coming soon in Medical Romance!

To
Anne Marie, Helen, Leanne, Raelene and Tracy
For *always* being available for lunch x

Dear Reader

A sexy Russian hero?

Yes, please!

How times have changed.

How much smaller the world is.

Levander Kolovsky, to me, is the ultimate hero. Without wishing to sound too gushing, I cannot tell you how much I adore him. So much so that when he was just a seed in my mind, when I hadn't even told my editor what I was thinking, I was chatting to my friend Vera about the latest man I couldn't get out of my head, and she turned and smiled and said, 'I'm Russian; well, my parents are—go for it—he sounds gorgeous.'

He is.

I am so thrilled to be here, and that *my* ultimate hero is part of Mills & Boon's one hundredth year celebration.

Enjoy

Carol x

CHAPTER ONE

THEY had to be breaking up, Millie decided.

Or rather *he* was breaking up with her.

To keep her brain from freezing over as she served patrons long into the night at the terribly exclusive Melbourne restaurant, Millie Andrews invented a background for each of the tables she waited on.

And now, as the clock edged past midnight, there were just three tables left.

One was a rather boozy celebratory business dinner, which thankfully, now that the bar was closed, was starting to wind up. The second consisted of a rather strained couple. The lady had duly eaten her way through fish and salad, minus dressing, and was clearly uncomfortable in her very tight black velvet dress. Millie decided she had probably just had a baby and was feeling horribly self-conscious at being out with her very good-looking but extremely passive-aggressive husband—'You don't really want dessert, do you, darling?'

And then there was the beautiful pair.

Blonde, svelte and jangling with nerves, a stunning woman was imploring her dining partner to 'just, please, listen'—reaching for his hand, her throaty voice urgent as her… Millie couldn't quite make this one out— husband, fiancé…? No neither fitted. Boyfriend? Or just lover, perhaps…? As he sat and listened impassively, utterly unmoved by her desperate pleas.

'Please, if you would just listen to me—really listen…'

They were too rich to notice or care that a waitress was clearing away their barely touched plates, and Millie's ears were on elastic as the blonde beauty begged for her chance, her bright, blue eyes glittering with tears as she choked the words out and reached for his hand again. 'Before you say it cannot happen, just hear what I have to say first…please.'

'Perhaps *you* should try listening…' he growled. His voice was accented, deep, low and just divine, but since till then the only words he'd growled in Millie's direction had been, 'Rare steak, fresh tomato salad,' so far she hadn't been able to place it. 'All night I have told you no, yet still you persist.'

'Why do you think I persist, Levander?'

Russian, Millie finally recognised, lingering rather too long over clearing the table. His salad had barely been touched; his steak was only half eaten. If she'd followed protocol, she should have asked then if everything had been to his satisfaction—if, by chance, there was a problem with his meal—but the intense conversation and his mood certainly didn't encourage interruption, and, given that it was her last night in Melbourne, protocol went where it belonged.

Straight out of the window.

'You persist because you hope I change my mind.

How many times do you have to hear me say it to understand that I never will?'

Even as she backed away, and even though the kitchen had long ago closed, Millie was tempted to offer them the dessert menu. Prepared even to whisk up dessert herself if it meant she could listen on.

They fascinated her.

Fascinated her.

From the second they had walked in she had been entranced.

By him.

As he'd walked through the door, standing tall, brooding and vaguely familiar in a charcoal suit, loosening his tie as his eyes scowled over the room, a low murmur had gone around and every head had turned—especially Millie's, as she'd tried and failed to place him. Ross, the manager, had raced over and steered them to the most private table at the back of the restaurant, then delivered Millie a quick warning before he dispatched her to take their orders.

'Nothing's too much trouble, okay?'

His date was beautiful, yes—on any other night she'd be a fascinating subject—but the glamorous woman faded into insignificance beside her date, because he was…

…exquisite.

As an artist Millie was often asked where her inspiration came from—and here was a fragment of the answer.

Inspiration came in the most unexpected places and at the most unexpected times. Twelve hours before she left Australia—twelve hours before she headed home for London—her head should be buzzing with "to do" lists. She should be adding up her tips and working out if she could afford the night in Singapore she'd booked *en route*. Instead she was consumed with this fascinating man—his beauty was, quite literally, inspiring.

His bone structure was impeccable, and his features had Millie's fingers aching to pull out a sketchpad and capture them: in perfect symmetry, as with all true beauties, his high cheekbones razored through his face, a strong jawline was dark and unshaven against his pale skin. His thick, longish hair was charcoal, not quite black, but too dark to be called brown, and whatever pallet his creator had used, the brush had been dipped twice in the same well—his eyes held the same bewitching hue, only deeper and glossier.

His date was gorgeous—possibly one of the most beautiful women Millie had seen—yet she dimmed beside him. The whole restaurant dimmed a touch, and she wanted to capture that, make him the sole focus—like endless Russian dolls, Millie mused, seeing the germ of the picture she would create in her mind's eye: him—the biggest most stunning, most exquisitely featured—and the rest—his date, the other clients, the staff, the street outside—ever diminishing objects, growing smaller and smaller till there was nothing left.

'You are a cold bastard.' His date hissed the words out, almost spat them across the table. But he didn't flinch and neither, Millie noted, did he attempt to dispute the fact.

'It must be hereditary.'

'So that's it? After all I've told you—you can just sit there?' Still he didn't answer—utterly bored, he had the audacity to yawn as she promptly burst into tears. 'You're not even going to think about it?'

Again he didn't answer, and even though Millie still hadn't managed to pin a label on her as, sobbing yet somehow elegant, the blonde stumbled out of the restaurant, it was clear that whatever her title had been a few minutes ago it had just been superseded. As of this moment she was an ex.

'She waits now for me to run after her…' Those charcoal eyes stared up at her, his lashes so thick, his gaze so intense, that for a second Millie's world stopped.

I'd wait, Millie thought, stunned that he was talking to her, that he didn't seem remotely embarrassed that she'd witnessed this intensely personal moment.

'I will sit here for a while longer—hopefully she will get the message and go home.'

'Or she might ring you on your mobile,' Millie said, blushing furiously as she did so, because even if it seemed to be idle conversation, as a lowly waitress it was inappropriate to comment. Management's orders were very clear: she should merely smile politely and move on.

Only she didn't.

Instead she hovered on the giddy line of propriety. His eyes pinned her, and the impact of him close up, of actually conversing with him, was utterly, fabulously devastating—and he surely knew it. Knew it because instead of looking away, instead of dismissing her, he responded with a question.

'Would you wait?'

'Perhaps…' Her voice when it came was breathy, her shirt suddenly impossibly tight as she struggled to drag air into her lungs, her skin on fire—and not because Ross, her manager, was looking on and frowning at the exchange. 'Once I'd calmed down, once I'd…' She didn't get to finish as, almost on cue, his phone rang. And at that point she crossed the line. Instead of turning and discreetly walking away, instead of heading back to the bar to let him take his call, she stood there, watching transfixed as he picked up his phone with long, pale, slender fingers that had Millie wondering if he was also an artist—wondering if that might be the reason she was so drawn to him.

'Thank you for the warning,' he said, turning off the phone.

'You're welcome,' Millie croaked, her cheeks flaming as attraction fully hit, and she was, for the first time, privy to that unscrupulous face breaking into a smile.

'Another.' He gestured to his glass, and Millie was about to say no, that the bar had closed about ten minutes ago. But glancing over to her boss, and seeing him frantically nodding, Millie gave a smile and, slipping away, headed over to the bar.

'What was that all about?' Ross asked the second she was within earshot.

'What?'

'Come on, Millie, don't play games with me. What was that cosy little exchange you were having with Levander?'

'He was just talking.' Millie flushed, and not just at being caught flirting—even his name was sexy. 'You were the one who said that nothing should be too much trouble. It would have been rude to walk away.'

'You know how to handle things.' Ross shot her a

warning look. 'Do you want me to take his drink over for you?'

'Of course not.' Millie shook her head, quickly changing the subject as Ross poured a generous dash of vodka into a glass. 'Should we get the port those businessmen wanted? They might get upset if they see us still serving him.'

'The bar's closed,' Ross said, placing the drink down for Millie to take over. 'At least to anyone who isn't a Kolovsky.'

'Kolovsky?' Mille frowned, trying to place the familiar name and hoping he'd elaborate, but Ross just grinned.

'It's Russian for money!'

Placing his drink in front of him, Millie was curiously disappointed when he didn't look up, when he didn't even give a distracted thanks. Instead he stared across the room and out onto the street, drumming his fingers restlessly. Never had it taken so long to place a drink on a table, to clear away a few stray glasses and wait—wait for him to bring her into his delicious focus, to once again, even for a moment, be the woman who held his attention.

Only he didn't.

'You might as well go home, Millie.' Ross came over as the last of the rowdy businessmen finally tipped out onto the street, but the words she'd been waiting to hear all night didn't sound quite so sweet now. Despite her tiredness, despite an empty suitcase waiting to be filled and a flight to be caught back to London in the morning, suddenly she didn't want to go. Staring over at the table, she watched as he leant back in his chair and took a slow sip of his drink. Ross did the same. 'I might as well get started on some paperwork—he looks as if he's settled for the night.'

Millie couldn't help but frown—an extra drink for a special customer was one thing, but for Ross to happily sit and while away an hour or two was unprecedented. This time Ross was only too happy to elaborate. 'He's a great tipper—as you're about to find out.' He held out a black velvet folder and peeled out an indecent amount of notes, taking his cut and handing the rest to Millie. 'Looks like you'll be staying in Singapore after all!'

'Goodness.'

'You deserve it. You've been a great worker—a real asset to the restaurant.' He went over to the till and handed her an envelope. 'There are your other tips and your wages, and there's a reference in there, too. If you're ever back in Melbourne, know that there's always a job here for you.'

More than anything Millie hated goodbyes. Ross wasn't even that much of a friend, but still tears filled her eyes as she took the envelope. Maybe it was emotion catching up, maybe it was the fact that no doubt she'd never be back, her dream trip to Australia to showcase her art having been nothing but a flop, but for whatever reason, she gave him a small hug.

Without this job she'd have been home weeks ago.

Without this job she'd still be wondering if she might have one day made it.

Like it or not, at least now she knew the answer.

There were a million things she had to do, but instead of turning left as she exited the restaurant Millie turned right, noisily clipping along Collins Street on black stilettos that needed re-heeling, barely even glancing into the exclusive shops as she headed to the gallery for one final glimpse of her work in the window.

And then she saw it. Millie's head turned so abruptly that she was positively whiplashed as she put a very beautiful face to a very beautiful name.

House of Kolovsky.

The cerulean blue frontage and the embossed gold lettering were familiar the world over—yet so far removed from Millie's existence that till now she'd barely even given the building a glance. Unable to resist now, though, she teetered forward, gazing into a magnificent window, dressed with ream after ream of the heavy silk that was so much the Kolovsky trademark, with opals as big as gulls' eggs seemingly casually tossed in—but the effect was so stunning Millie was in no doubt that each jewel had been placed with military precision, along with the tiny lights that were twinkling and catching the fluid colour of the fabric.

Kolovsky was renowned for its stunning fashion collections as well as the fabrics themselves: rich, heavy silks that were supposed to have the same magical effect as opals—capturing the light and even, it was rumoured by devotees, changing colour according to a woman's mood. Millie had raised her eyebrows in rather bored disbelief when she'd read that in a magazine, but standing with her nose practically against the window, seeing the heavy, fabulous tones and sumptuous attention to detail, Mille could almost believe it. What she was finding rather more difficult to fathom, though, was what had taken place earlier. She had flirted with none other than Levander Kolovsky.

She *had* seen him before—it was all coming to her now: notorious bad boy, the darling of the tabloids here in Melbourne, his every move, his every comment, his every encounter faithfully and libellously documented.

Millie let out a gurgle of laughter. She'd been flirting with the biggest rake in Melbourne. Just wait till she told Anton!

Peeling herself away from the window, Millie allowed herself just one final glimpse. She would have loved to feel her body draped in something so exquisite. Not that she could ever afford it. Millie sighed, picking up her pace and walking the few doors down to the gallery. She could barely afford anything at the moment— which was how a tortured artist was supposed to start, Mille reminded herself. But her usual pep-talk was starting to lose its oomph—cold reality hitting home as she stood on the pavement outside the gallery.

Very soon she wouldn't be a struggling artist.

Instead she'd be a teacher.

Seeing a light on inside, Millie stood well back, not wanting Anton, the owner, to see her tears as she bade goodbye to her dream.

'Which one is yours?' How long she'd stood there staring Millie had no idea. She'd been so lost in her own world she hadn't noticed someone approaching, hadn't heard him next to her. Only now that he was, every nerve sizzled with awareness.

'That one.' Millie pointed to a tiny oil painting with a shaking hand, wondering what his take would be. It was a field of flowers and grass, every blade smiling, every flower wearing a different expression, and in the middle was a wooden child bearing no features—it was quite simply her favourite piece, evoking for Millie such emotion and memory that it would truly break her heart if it ever did sell. Yet it was the one she had hoped would launch her career.

'Were you on drugs when you painted this?'

'No.' Millie let out a little laugh, not just at the question but at the pronunciation. His English, though excellent, was laced with a heavy dash of fabulous accent, and that he could make such an offensive remark sound somehow sexy was certainly a credit to him.

She glanced over at him. His face was at the window, and he was peering at her work with a frown. For an artist it was actually a compliment—someone trying to fathom her work, instead of a brief, cursory glance and then on to the next one.

'My brother's autistic—when I was younger I remember the doctor explaining to me that the reason he didn't cuddle or kiss or show affection was because of the way he saw the world. The clouds, the trees, the grass and animals were in his eyes just as important as us—to him, people were the inanimate objects. That's me.' She pointed to the frozen lifeless object in the middle, waited for his comment. For an age it didn't come. He was looking, really looking, at her picture.

'I knew a child once—he screamed if he had to go to bed. Not just screamed...' Slate eyes turned to hers and Millie was lost. 'Every night it was as if he was ter-

rified. Do you think to him the bed was real? That perhaps he thought he would hurt it…?'

'Maybe.' Millie was flustered, wondering who he
was referring to, wanting to know more. But it didn't
matter anyway. The fact that her work had provoked
such thought, a memory, such a question, was reward
enough in itself. 'I don't know, but I guess it's possible.'

'And may I ask the name of the artist?'

'You may. It's Millie.' She smiled. 'Millie Andrews.'

'Your accent?' He frowned just as Millie had when
trying to place his. 'England? London?'

'That's right.'

'Are you here on holiday?'

'A working holiday…' Millie gave a rueful smile. 'I
go home tomorrow.'

'Shame.'

She'd been flirted with on many occasions, but never
so blatantly and never by anyone so divine.

'Millie?' He pondered on her name for a moment. 'I
am not familiar with that. Is it short for something?'

'Do we have to go there?'

'Sorry?'

'Millicent.' She winced. 'My parents must have
been—' She didn't get to finish. Anton was frantically
waving in recognition as he came to the window, gesturing for her to come inside. It would have been rude
to say no, to shake her head and carry on this delicious
conversation. So, extremely reluctantly, she turned to
bid Levander goodnight.

Clearly he had other ideas. As the door opened, instead of walking away, instead of concluding their time

together, he blatantly extended it, moving to the door, then stepping back to allow her to go first, his hand taking her elbow. It wasn't just his boldness that startled Millie but the contact itself—the firm, warm, incredibly male contact that had her more flustered than she cared, or rather dared to admit.

'Ready for the off?' Anton's effeminate voice rang out as he scooped her into a hug, but it lasted about point three of a second. He dropped her like a hot coal as he clapped eyes on her companion.

'My, my, Millie. And I thought you were supposed to be working tonight.'

'I—I am.' Millie stammered. 'I was. Anton, this is…'

'I know who it is.' Anton beamed. 'Welcome, welcome, Levander—and may I say I just love your new range?'

'It is not my range.' Levander smiled tightly. 'I deal with the business, not the fashion.'

'Well, I adore it anyway,' Anton gushed, but Levander wasn't listening. Instead he wandered around the gallery, squinting as he peered closely at the paintings, some holding his attention, others barely meriting a cursory glance.

'Do you know him?' Millie whispered, which was more than a touch rude, but she just had to know more about him.

'Everyone knows who the Kolovskys are.'

'I mean do you *know* him?'

'I wish,' Anton sighed. 'The boutique may be a couple of doors down from me—but the Kolovskys are a million miles away. I did used to talk to the twins, though…' Anton smiled at her frown. 'They're just as gorgeous. Millie have you any idea who you're dealing with? They're practically royalty here,' Anton breathed, 'and your beau tonight is first in line.'

His voice trailed off as Levander made his way back to them, and Anton spectacularly saved the rather awkward moment, rolling his eyes dramatically at Levander. 'I'm scolding Millie for even considering being seen with you in her waitress garb. Mind you, perhaps it's just as well— I assume you've seen her when she's not working?'

'Not yet.' Levander turned and gave Millie a slow, lingering look, unashamedly undressing her with his eyes for an indecent amount of time as she stood there squirming. Not even turning back to Anton, he carried on talking. 'But I am very much looking forward to it.'

'Well, don't get too excited,' Anton sighed. 'Millie has no end of paint-splattered shorts and T-shirts, but not much else.'

'I see you have only one of Millie's paintings in the window—while other artists there have two.'

'The other artists have sold.' Anton held his palms up to the air in a helpless gesture. 'Actually, Millie, darling…' He gave a little wince. 'I'm not going to take you out of the gallery, but space is at a premium, and with this new exhibition I'm going to have to move—'

'You have more of Millie's work?' Levander interrupted. 'I would like to see it if I may.'

'Of course.' Anton gave Millie a wide-eyed look as he gestured him to the back of the gallery, to the tiny piece of wall that—for now at least—displayed her work.

'Your price is too low…' Levander ran a quick eye through Millie's bio and gave a shake of his head. 'And you come across too needy—too grateful that anyone should even stop to look at your work, let alone buy it. You need to raise your price.'

'It was higher,' Millie answered, 'and I still didn't sell.'

'This is an exclusive gallery—yes?' Levander waited for Anton's hesitant nod. 'People do not want rubbish on their walls—and at this price that is what they think they are buying.'

'She's an unknown.' Anton's bubbly demeanour dimmed a touch as his judgement was challenged, but Levander held firm.

'*Today* she is unknown.' He turned to Millie. 'Change it before you leave. Rewrite your bio…' He turned the page. 'Each painting is now the cost of your air ticket— the price you paid to share your talent.'

'It won't work…'

'So you have lost nothing. And she should have at least two in the window…'

'Levander…' Anton was blushing, flirting, and trying to be assertive all at the same time. 'Millie's already had three months on display in the window. I simply cannot—'

'When is this exhibition you mentioned?' Levander interrupted. 'I remember my stepmother saying she wanted another nice piece for the boutique. Perhaps I should suggest that she comes for a look?'

'I already sent an invite,' Anton said dubiously, 'and as usual it was politely declined.'

'Nina wouldn't have even seen it,' Levander said dismissively. 'It would have been her assistant who declined on her behalf. If I tell her about it myself, I can assure you she will come—and possibly my father, too. Though I am not sure if *I* will be available.'

Anton was right—clearly Millie hadn't a clue. Because at just the hint that they were coming to the preview Anton was a gibbering wreck, promptly dispatching her to choose another piece to go in the window before a "bored now" Levander took her by the hand and led her outside.

'You—You didn't have to do that…' Millie stammered, once they were out on the street.

'No one *has* to do anything.' Levander shrugged. 'Your work deserves its chance.'

'Thank you.' Millie shook her head to clear it. 'Your stepmother *will* go to the exhibition?' she checked. 'I mean, if she's already declined… I'd hate for Anton to be disappointed—especially if he's giving me so much of a prime position. He's already been more than generous…'

'She will be there,' Anton said assuredly. 'She will not want to go, of course. But when I tell her she is expected—that I have accepted on her behalf—she will have no choice but to go.'

'Sorry?'

'It would appear rude to not turn up—and in my family appearance is everything.'

'Well, thank you…' Millie said. 'You've no idea how much it means.'

'I have a very good idea what it means,' Levander corrected her. 'I know how important that first sale is—and, yes, I could have bought your painting—given you the red dot on your work for the world to see—but that would be cheating, yes?'

On so many levels, Millie realised, staring up at him. His skin was white in the street light, contrasting with the hollow shadows of his cheeks, his eyes two dark, unreadable pools.

'It will sell—some things that are truly beautiful don't always catch the eye first time around.' Levander's voice was a caress. 'Sometimes you need to actually stop and take another look.'

He was certainly taking a good look now. His gaze was so intense, his face so close she could feel the heat of his breath on her face. She thought for a blissful second that he was going to kiss her, but instead it was his rich deep voice that bathed her senses, his eyes quizzical as they assessed her. 'So, you leave tomorrow?'

'In the morning.'

'And have you enjoyed your time in Melbourne?'

'I haven't really seen anything of it.' She gave a tiny shrug. 'I've been to a few galleries, a couple of shows—but mainly I've been working...' Her voice trailed off, her simple answer somehow giving him an opening she'd never intended. Millie's breath caught in her throat as Levander took it.

'Then we'd better get started. Come...' He pointed to where a pony and trap was pulling in across the deserted street, tourists climbing down, the weary trap rider about to dismantle and head off home. He shook his head when Levander called for him to wait.

'Sorry, mate. That was the last ride for the night—back again tomorrow.'

'I will talk with him.' Levander turned to go, but she shook her head.

'It doesn't matter. It's late…' Millie attempted, struggling in quicksand as she stared into his eyes. 'And I've got a plane to catch tomorrow…'

'Plenty of time to sleep on the plane, then.'

But a blip of sensibility was invading now. She was playing with fire here, and her assessment was based on not just what she had read—Anton himself had warned her, and Levander's own dining companion hadn't exactly given him a glowing reference.

'You're a cold bastard.'

The pain in her voice had been real, the emotion that had choked out those words hadn't been manufactured— and Levander's response had done little to dispute the accusation.

What the hell was she doing?

It would be madness to go with this man.

'Really…' Millie swallowed hard. 'It's probably not such a good idea. I've got so much to do, and you—well you…'

'Don't worry about me.'

'You just broke up with your girlfriend, Levander…' She wasn't going to play games. 'You're probably feeling a bit…'

'You have no idea how I am feeling…' Instead of walking away, he stepped closer, took her face in his hands, his warm skin actually cool on her stinging cheeks. 'And I did not break up with my girlfriend— Annika is my half-sister…'

'It was your *half-sister* you were rowing with?'

Levander nodded, his eyes narrowing. 'What did you hear?'

'Nothing.' Millie blushed. The only thing she had heard was that he was a cold bastard, but she could hardly tell him that. 'I just saw her flounce off.'

'And that is all?'

After a beat of hesitation she nodded.

'Siblings fight.' His breath mingled with hers, and that cynical mouth was so close Millie could almost taste it—like a chocolate cake cooking in the oven, teasing her senses…

'She's really your half-sister?' Millie checked, wanting to believe him but scared to at the same time. Wanting him to kiss her but worried that he would.

'Who else would I allow to talk to me like that?' Levander answered. 'Now, you wait here.'

What had she heard?

Levander's hackles were raised, his mind, eternally vigilant, racing as he recalled not just his conversation with Annika, but the times Millie had been present.

At first he'd barely noticed her—a waitress not meriting even a glance from him, especially with the tense subject matter that had been forcing his attention—and then she'd moved to clear his plate.

Her heavenly scent had reached him, her tiny embarrassed smile as she'd caught his eyes, and from that second on he'd thanked her for the distraction—thanked this unknown woman who had allowed his mind to detour as Annika delivered the fatal news and shrilled the family's demands.

So much more pleasant to stare over Annika's shoulder and watch the woman, the pink flush on her cheeks, her blonde curls tumbling further out of their hair tie with each swoosh through the kitchen door, her slight exasperation as she dealt with a rowdy table. He had felt surprising pleasure as he'd watched that full, pretty mouth nibble on the end of her pen between writing down orders. And later, when still Annika had persisted, when it had all been just too much to deal with—his battle to remain outwardly calm despite the emotions churning within—it had been a welcome relief when she'd returned to his table. Her soft fragrance had been such a contrast to the bitter musk of the Kolovsky perfume Annika had doused herself in—a delicate hint of vanilla and something he couldn't define, like a breath of fresh air—and as she'd leant forward to clear his table he'd tried and failed not to notice the slight tug of her blouse as it strained over her breasts. He had actually had to look away when she'd stooped to retrieve a dropped napkin and he'd caught a glimpse of the creamy flesh of her cleavage.

He wanted her.

Handing the rider a sizeable wad of notes, he bought them a little more time—but somehow he knew it wasn't enough. That if he made a move too soon—she'd run like a squirrel up a tree.

And yet if it was sex he wanted there were easier ways. He could head back to the hotel, return any one of the endless messages that would undoubtedly be on his answering machine and lose himself tonight.

How he wanted to lose himself.

Like a judge summing up, he bitterly assessed the conversation that had taken place with Annika—the family demands that had been delivered by the sweetest, the most vulnerable of them all.

His father was dying.

Which, according to the family, meant there was now no question of Levander leaving—no question of him turning his back on the people who had apparently given him everything he possessed.

Five more years of hell was what they were demanding.

Levander had gritted his teeth at the prospect, but the sentencing hadn't ended there—a wife and child had been added to the non-parole period.

Well, they could all go to hell!

He'd more than served his time—he had saved the House of Kolovsky from financial suicide almost the second he'd joined the firm. That they now had the audacity to think he actually owed them anything made Levander's stomach churn with loathing.

To think that that bastard, after all he had done—

'Hey.' Her sweet voice broke into his black thoughts, her smiling, trusting face such an engaging contrast with the hard-nosed women he was too used to dealing with. 'Did you manage to persuade him?'

'Of course,' Levander answered calmly, though his mind was anything but. 'I am a very good persuader.' He watched her eyes widen a touch, registered the tiny nervous swallow in her throat at the slightly provocative statement, and so badly he wanted to kiss her—to push that soft body against a wall, to press his lips to hers, to feel her soft, fragrant skin beneath his hands, to take her up to his hotel and make love to her…

To somehow take refuge from the savage sleet of his thoughts… But strangely, for Levander, it wasn't *all* he wanted from her.

For the first time Levander wanted more than the passion of a woman to fill his night.

He wanted her company.

CHAPTER TWO

IT WAS the strangest first date she'd ever been asked on—but one thing was sure: it *was* a date.

Millie knew that—knew from the way he was looking at her and the fact that she couldn't stop looking at him—knew from the butterflies dancing in her stomach and the shrill of pleasure that there was definitely romance in the air.

If it had been with anyone else a romantic horse and cart ride around the city would have been tacky, but with Levander it didn't feel that way. With the feel of the cool night air on her cheeks, the noise of the horse as it clipped through the semi-deserted streets and the warmth of Levander by her side it felt amazing. It was a whirlwind Monopoly board tour of Melbourne. They clopped past Flinders Street Station, the famous old building stunning by night and lit up like a fairground, and Levander pointed out the sights as they went, from a vibrant Southbank that was still awake despite the hour, and the casino glittering and beckoning, to the smart theatre district and lavish hotels at the top end of town.

'This is where I live.'

He had to lean into her to say it. Her skirt had already ridden up a touch, and, feeling his suited thigh against her bare one, it was almost all she could do to look up instead of down. Her whole focus was on his body against hers.

'It's a hotel.'

'Up there,' Levander elaborated. 'On the top floor.'

'You actually *live* there?'

'Why not?'

He stared down at her and she forgot her question, sure he was about to kiss her. She almost wept in frustration when the cart halted somewhat abruptly, lurching them both backwards into their seats, but Levander gave a small lazy smile as he climbed out—a smile that told her there was plenty of time for that later. And as he stepped down and took her hand to help her down, just his touch confirmed what they both knew.

There *would* be a later.

'You like to dance?'

'No,' Millie admitted, gulping as they descended steep stairs into a tiny smoky and very exclusive private club that she wouldn't have known existed even if she'd been walking on the street outside.

Exclusive because only the most beautiful or famous seemed to be present—faces that had Millie frowning as she tried to place them, then jolting in recognition as the social pages she devoured in magazines came to life before her very eyes.

'Do you?'

'Sometimes.' Levander shrugged, pushing her through the crowd with one arm around her.

The slow, heavy thud of the music was out of time with her rapidly beating heart as he led her to a small, plush impossibly sexy booth that was clearly designed for intimacy. Like some erotic confessional, the purple velvet-lined seats went up to the ceiling, dulling the chatter and noise enough to allow conversation so long as one leant forward. And as he sat opposite her the table was so narrow it was impossible not to touch knees—impossible to look anywhere but at him.

He ordered their drinks—didn't even ask her what she wanted—and some strange red cocktail appeared that tasted icy and delicious, burning her throat and stomach as she sipped it. But it didn't compare to the sensations Levander evoked.

'Relax,' he ordered, as if she should be able to on command. Only Millie couldn't.

Even here, amongst Melbourne's most beautiful, Levander caused a stir—she'd seen the ripple effect wash through the crowd as they'd walked to their table. Like a mini Mexican wave going through the bar, heads had turned and conversations had paused; Millie had half expected oxygen masks to drop from the ceiling as every female sucked in her stomach *en masse*—but all eyes were most definitely on Levander. His questionable choice of date tonight didn't even merit a second uninterested glance.

Clearly there'd be a new one tomorrow.

Clearly every woman present hoped it might be them.

'You are here to sell paintings, I take it, not for a holiday?'

'That was the plan,' Millie sighed.

'So why are you going back now?'

'I gave myself three months. It was Anton who suggested I come out here.'

'You knew Anton before you came?'

'I met him last year, when he was in London.' Millie nodded. 'I was just finishing my degree and he came as a guest speaker.'

'He is not an artist?' Levander checked.

'No—but he's extremely well known for showcasing new talent, and I was fortunate because he liked my work. We got on well, and he said if I was ever interested in coming over… So here I am—at least until tomorrow. I really can't afford to stay on any longer.'

He pulled back just enough to squint down at his watch. 'It is already tomorrow,' Levander pointed out. 'So what happens now—when you go back, I mean? If your work is not selling…'

'I studied teaching as well.' Millie sighed at the prospect. 'As something to fall back on. I suppose it's just as well I did.'

'You can do both,' Levander pointed out. 'Just because you cannot make a living from your art, it does not mean that you have to give it up completely.'

'I know that.' Millie sighed again. 'It's just…' her voice faded. Melancholy musings were not really the correct form for a first date, but Levander pushed her to continue and, given that nothing about tonight had even bordered on normal, Millie decided to tell him—to reveal just a little more of herself than she otherwise might. 'When I work…well, it's sort of hot and cold. Yes, in theory it would be fabulous to work Monday to

Friday, and save my art for the weekends and evenings—I know it's what a lot of people do—but…'

'But?'

'The picture you saw tonight?' Millie said, and Levander nodded. 'It was sort of brewing in my head for a couple of weeks, and finally—when I could see it, when I was actually ready to put my vision onto the canvas—I locked myself away for a more than a week. I just can't imagine that I'd ever have done that piece if I'd had to slot in the real world. My focus is totally on my art; it's like I just turn on and everything else is off. Except for occasionally surfacing for food and showers I just live and breathe to paint. Actually…' she gave a tiny embarrassed giggle '…come to think about it, nutrition and hygiene weren't exactly at the top of my agenda.'

And if that revelation wasn't correct form either, Levander didn't seem to mind a bit. In fact he leant closer, if that were possible, so close she could feel his breath on her cheek, could feel his knee and the lower part of his thigh against hers as he dizzied her with his thoughts.

'Now you are *really* turning me on!'

Shocked, wondering if she'd misheard, misunderstood, perhaps, Millie tipped back a fraction, wide eyes meeting his, flushing under his lazy scrutiny as he told her without a word that she hadn't misheard.

'Do you come here a lot?' Millie croaked, taking a desperate slug of her drink and wondering if she'd been spirited into a very early menopause as for the millionth time that evening a hot flush sent another searing blush up to her face. The heat between them was so stifling surely someone must have turned off the

air-conditioner—and had there been a menu handy
Millie would have grabbed it as a fan.

'Occasionally,' Levander answered easily—so pale
and elegant and utterly calm it made her want to weep
at the injustice. His eyes shifted momentarily as he
glanced at the beautiful crowd. 'But really I don't like
it much: too many people with empty minds who think
they are interesting.'

'Oh.'

He mesmerised her—every word reeling her in,
every feature captivating her. How long she stared, how
long they held eye contact, Millie had no idea—but it
seemed to go on for ever. Another entirely separate conversation was taking place, without a single word, and
though his eyes never left hers, though his hands were
safely on the table, he might just as well have been
touching her—because her body seared at his beckoning, the dull red of her cheeks stealing down over her
bosom as still they didn't speak, blood fizzing through
her veins. It seemed to engorge her body, swelling her
most feminine places. Her nipples were thrumming
against her flimsy blouse as somewhere deep inside—
low, so low in her stomach—a delicious knot tightened.
Her panties were damp now as still he stared on. She
couldn't move, didn't dare even to run a dry tongue
over her lips so intense was the arousal, and all Millie
knew was that if she didn't break the spell, didn't literally force herself to speak, then she'd surely lean over
and kiss him, or take him by the hand and run...

'How long have you been in Melbourne?' Her voice
was a croak.

'Does it matter?' Still he stared.

'Do you like your work?' Millie attempted vainly.

'Is this a job interview?' He was watching her mouth intently now, making it almost impossible to form a sentence. God what did this man do to her? With one look she was a shivering mass of lust—and with one crook of his finger, Millie knew, she'd follow him gladly to wherever he wanted to take her. It both excited and terrified her. Supremely cautious with men, supremely cautious with her emotions, it was as if she had suddenly dropped the rule book she'd lived her life by in the bath, leaving its pages damp and illegible, all its moral guidelines so deeply entrenched utterly indecipherable in Levander's heady presence.

She wanted him to make love to her—wanted him now, this very minute. Wanted him to take her out of this bar, take her anywhere, just so long as he ravished her…

…wanted him to be her first.

Oh, she hadn't held on to her virginity for some prudish reason—work, study, the strains of family life had meant she'd never let anyone particularly close, had never actually invested the energy to take a relationship to that next level, had never trusted another enough to give that part of herself.

But she'd give it to Levander.

In a heartbeat.

And that thought alone shocked her to the very core.

'I came to Australia as a teenager.' Levander's voice broke her introspection, broke the sensual spell. Maybe he had sensed the shift in her, the shock that had ricocheted through her, but suddenly things were, if not normal, then safer, and her mind scrambled to remember the question she had first voiced. 'I studied finance and business—as well as learning English, of course.'

'You didn't speak English when you came?'

'Not a word.'

'Your brothers and sisters here spoke Russian, though?' Millie checked, appalled at how it must have been for him to land in a family and not even be able to communicate.

'*Half*-brothers and sisters,' Levander corrected. 'And, no, they did not speak much Russian. But language was the least of our barriers.'

'What do you mean?'

'We had different childhoods.' Levander flicked away the question with his hand, then reached for a drink. But even if he wanted that part of the conversation over, even if clearly she'd wandered into forbidden territory, Millie wanted to know more.

'What about your mother?' Millie asked, remembering that here he had a stepmother. 'Do you get back to see her? Is she still in Russia?'

'She is dead.' Just like that he said it—his expression not changing, his voice completely even—as if the detail was so trivial it was hardly worth a mention. 'So there is no reason at all to go back. As I was saying, when I finished my degree I assumed the role of Financial Director at the House of Kolovsky.'

'It must be quite a job.' Millie blinked. 'I mean, the name's everywhere.'

'We have outlets all over the world. Melbourne is really just kept on for sentimental reasons—this is where my father came when he emigrated from Russia. Our main outlets are in Europe, and of course the US, so I travel a lot—which is good.'

'Must be interesting?'

'Sometimes.' Levander shrugged. 'But the people in the industry leave a lot to be desired.' He curled his lip and made a small hissing sound. 'It is full of bitches— and I am not only talking about the women. It is the most narcissistic environment to be in. Like here—' His hand gestured to the heaving room. 'Everyone here would happily claim to be my best friend—would that be the case if I worked in a lower profile job?'

'I don't know…' Millie mused. Because even if the answer was seemingly obvious—even if his position *must* ensure a never-ending stream of hangers-on—long before she'd known his name, in fact from the second Millie had laid eyes on him, she'd been captivated. And from Millie's perspective it wasn't hard to afford others the benefit of the doubt. 'You can't know that either…' She gave a helpless shrug, not sure how she could tell him that even if he took away the suit, the money, the name—he was still far and away the most exciting, breathtaking company she'd ever kept.

'I *do* know, though,' Levander said firmly. 'From the day I set foot in Australia I have had endless friends—yet no one wanted to know me when I was a Detsky Dom kid.'

'Detsky Dom?' Millie frowned. 'Is that where you're from?'

It was an innocent question, clarifying things in her own mind as she pieced together his history. She expected him to nod, to just say yes and move on. But instead those brooding features shifted into a wry smile, and she didn't know if it was her attempt at pronunciation or if he was laughing at some sort of private joke.

'That is right, Millie—I am from *Detsky Dom*. Come…' Standing abruptly, he offered her hand. 'You do not belong here—let's go somewhere where we can properly talk.'

Which was easier said than done. As he guided her through the throng, his hand on her waist, his broad shoulders acting as a buffer, his name was called from every direction. Not that he deigned to respond—even when a rather ravishing Latina woman grabbed him by the sleeve of his jacket, Levander merely shrugged her off.

'Levander, please…' She caught up with them just as they stepped out of the lobby. Millie's foot was almost on the pavement outside when her tearful voice pleaded her case. 'You cannot walk out like this… We made love last night—please talk to me.'

Which was a pretty good case to plead, Millie thought, as with a grim half-smile Levander excused himself and led the dark beauty to a corner of the lobby—leaving Millie to stand making polite small talk with the doorman. Her cheeks burned with humiliation—not just because of the paper tissue way he clearly treated women, not just because she was obviously the next one in the box, but because of the very fact she wasn't walking away.

It was hell to watch.

Like some gory bit in a film, where you wanted to peek from behind a cushion, it was just horrible, listening to her plead her case, begging him for another chance, promising to change and more. But far worse for Millie was Levander's response—not cool and detached, as she'd expected, instead he bordered on sympathetic, seeming understanding of her plight even as he patiently explained why he hadn't returned her calls and reiterated what he had already told her—that it was over.

Still, when her glittering eyes fell on Millie, when a few choice words were said, his Latina lover must have crossed Levander's questionable line of moral conduct—because he stalked off, taking Millie firmly by the arm and leading her out onto the street.

'Levander…' the brunette sobbed. 'We need to talk.'

'What is the point?' Levander snarled, and never had his Russian accent been more pronounced as he bundled Millie into a taxi. 'When you're too drunk to remember what was said in the morning?'

'I'm sorry you had to see that.' They'd ended up at St Kilda Beach, and as they wandered along the foreshore it was the first time since the incident that either of them had spoken.

'Perhaps it's better that I did,' Millie answered tightly—the sobbing spectacle had been a rather timely reminder of what she'd almost let herself in for.

'We went out for a few weeks—but we were having problems…'

'Clearly you weren't having too many problems last night,' she sniffed.

He had the nerve to laugh at her response. The bloody nerve to *laugh!*

'Stop it,' Millie demanded. 'That's completely irredeemable….' Only it wasn't; Levander was so unashamedly bad, his behaviour so utterly and completely reprehensible, that inexplicably after a moment or two Millie was laughing too. Oh, not out loud laughing— but a very reluctant smile was wobbling on her lips as he took her in his arms. The whole thing was so awful, so far from anything she'd ever experienced, it was either that…

…or cry.

'Millie, I do not as a rule have…er…*problems* in that department. But Carla was wrong when she said we had made love last night.'

'I don't need the details…'

'In fact, though last night wasn't lacking in physicality, I could say that Carla and I, while we enjoyed each other, never "made love".'

'Please.' Millie closed her eyes against his gaze— because that wasn't the concern right now. Here she stood, with the most beautiful man she had ever met, listening as he told her, quite clearly, that he, unlike others, had no trouble separating sex from love—which should make perfect sense. After all, nestled in the club, feeling his legs pressing against her, all she had wanted was him, and love surely hadn't entered the equation…

Love *couldn't* have entered the equation because she barely knew him…

And yet…

Troubled eyes opened on his—and he was still there, still just as divine, still just as confusing.

'I am sorry…' His breath mingled with hers, his lips

a mere fraction away, and she stiffened, terrified of the dizzying effect he had on her. But somehow she didn't relax when he broke contact—when, extremely frustratingly, he became the perfect gentleman.

He talked politely as they walked towards the pier, occasionally taking her elbow when the moon dipped behind a cloud. Millie couldn't decide if she was either totally misreading the signs and he didn't fancy her a jot, if he was literally giving her a guided tour of Melbourne, or he was an absolute master in seduction. But by the time they neared the pier every cell in her body was quivering, every nerve taut with arousal. The skin on her bare arms flared as he took her forearm and turned her around. Surely now, Millie begged to herself, her lips aching with want, surely now he would kiss her. Only his simmering tease wasn't quite over. Turning the burner down just a touch, even as Millie's want bubbled near the edge, he guided her back into a public place.

It was the strangest place to bring someone.

A seamy café in the red light district of Melbourne— a rather odd choice for a date. But Levander, Millie realised, truly seemed to fit in anywhere. Whether at an exclusive bar or an all-night café, he had that supreme confidence combined with something else that Millie couldn't quite define. The café's owner greeted him by name as Levander guided her to a table and then went over to order. As she sat, anxious and awkward amidst the tired sex workers who were taking a well-earned break, the street kids trying to make one coffee last for ever, Millie wondered why the hell he'd brought her here. How anyone could relax in a place like this was beyond her.

'The coffee is great here,' Levander said, as if in answer, placing two steaming mugs and two large cakes on the table. 'I come her sometimes when I cannot sleep— not for *that* reason.' He smiled at her disapproving expression. 'It actually reminds me of home. There was an all-night café opposite the…' He hesitated just a fraction and Millie frowned. 'There was a café like this opposite where I lived. Sometimes when I cannot sleep I come here and watch the sun rise; it is a good place for thinking.'

'But surely…?' Millie started, and then stopped herself. But Levander clearly guessed what was on her mind—surely this was the last place a person could relax.

'They are good people too, Millie. They have to work, like all of us. You should not be so quick to judge.'

'I wasn't,' Millie answered indignantly, and then felt guilty—because that was exactly what she had been doing. She had looked around her with less than an open mind.

'It is rare that anyone disturbs me—they value their time alone, and they seem to respect that I value mine. And, as I said, the coffee is good.'

'So are these,' Millie said, finally relaxing a bit now, biting into the pastry and closing her eyes as the cool sweet custard melted on her tongue. 'So, what do you sit here and think about?'

'At the moment—work.'

'Because you're so busy?'

'Because I am thinking of leaving.'

'Oh.' Pastry forgotten, it hovered in her hand as Millie's eyes widened. 'What do your family say?'

'I haven't told them yet.' He gave a small smile as her pastry dropped to the table when Millie realised she was actually the only person privy to this particular plan. 'And it is not a prospect I relish. They will tell me I have commitments—they won't want to lose me. I have saved the company from ruin and made them plenty of money since I came.'

'How?' Millie asked. 'How did you save it?'

He didn't answer at first—made no secret of the fact he was weighing her up, deciding whether or not he should answer. But after what seemed like a lifetime he nodded, inviting her a shade deeper into his magical circle, and Millie leant in gratefully—not so much for what she might hear, but because perhaps he had decided to reveal more of himself to her.

'That is for another time.'

'There can't be another time…' She almost wept with frustration at his tease, at the hand of fate that had granted her this unexpected encounter but with such a cruel timeline. 'You know I go home tomorrow.'

'Don't you want to stay?'

Oh, *how* she wanted to. So badly she wanted to say yes. The minutes they had were ticking away as loudly as a kitchen timer, and her heart was dreading the buzz that would signal the bitter end. But she had no choice.

He gave her a tiny glimpse of what she would be missing—his hand leaving the safety of the table, his fingers toying with a loose strand of her hair. His flesh was not even touching hers, but she could feel the heat from his palm and she wanted to rest her face in it, wanted contact so much it actually hurt.

'We all have commitments,' Millie breathed, faint now with longing. 'Even me.'

'Pity.'

He watched as she nervously licked her lips, his eyes squinting slightly just as they had when he'd looked at the paintings, and Millie wondered if she had what it took to hold his attention, or if afterwards he'd simply move on.

'You know,' he mused out loud, 'for an industry that is supposed to promote beauty, the fashion industry can be very ugly. To them, you would not be considered beautiful…' Only someone like him could make it a compliment—especially now that he was touching her, caressing her cheek with his finger, tracing it down her face and along her neck, almost as if he were drawing her, the pad of his fingers cool on her throat, resting a moment on her rapid, leaping pulse. 'The face, yes. But the body…' She gave a small nervous swallow as his fingers swept along her shoulder, dusting her bare arms; all the tiny hairs standing up to attention as their mistress shivered. 'You are too much woman.'

'Is that another word for fat?' Millie gave a slightly shrill giggle. 'I know I should go to the gym more—I mean, I pay my membership…' She was blabbering now, seriously so. Oh, she wasn't fat—not even particularly overweight—but maybe compared to the reed-thin beauties Levander was used to…

Her thought process halted there. Transfixed, nervous, she watched as he leant over and undid the top button of her blouse. No one turned, not a single person in the café gave a damn. She could feel the top of her cleavage exposed, feel his eyes burning into her pale flesh. If it had been anyone or anywhere else she'd have slapped him—would have got up and walked out. Only it wasn't anyone else…

…it was Levander.

Jerking her eyes to his, Millie couldn't read them—was unsure of what to make of him. Unsure whether his words demoted or promoted her. Unsure of what Levander could possibly *need* from someone like her. She knew for sure now that she was wanted—knew for sure now where the night was leading…only an argument was brewing at the counter. Loud voices crudely interrupted this sensual moment as a young man, clearly the worse for wear, pulled out his pockets, trying to find money he'd never had to pay for a two a.m. breakfast that he'd already eaten. It was clearly the norm for this place—no one bar Millie and Levander was even looking up at the distraction.

'I musssht have dropped it…' the guy was slurring.

'Hey,' Levander called, standing up, and not for the first time during this crazy night Millie felt anxious—here she was in the seamiest of cafés, with a virtual stranger for company and a fight about to break out. She held her breath as Levander stood up and headed straight into the thick of things, blinking rapidly as he pulled out his wallet.

'You did drop it…'

He pulled out his wallet and handed the owner a note that would more than cover his breakfast. 'I found this on the pavement outside—perhaps I should give it to Jack to look after.'

'I want the change…' the guy slurred, but Levander shook his head.

'Tomorrow you will be hungry again. It is better Jack has it.' And without another word he headed back to Millie—who didn't know whether to be touched by his kindness or furious at his stupidity for getting involved.

'Nice place,' Millie said darkly, and almost instantly regretted it—especially when she saw Levander's face.

'You prefer five-star?' Levander shrugged. 'Prefer pompous men drunk on malt whisky who have lost their gold credit card, perhaps, than some poor kid who probably hasn't eaten in two days?'

Though she bristled at his implication, she refused to back down. 'He could have had a knife—he could have…' She shook her head in exasperation. 'And what happens when the money you gave the owner runs out, Levander? What happens next week, when you're not here to fix it for him?'

'For the next few nights he eats.' Levander shrugged.

'But when the money runs out the same thing will happen, and you won't be here…' Millie insisted.

But Levander neither needed nor wanted her take on things. In fact it would seem Levander no longer wanted her. Because suddenly, not for the first time that night, he stood up to go, taking her hand and without a word hailing a taxi from the rank outside, giving his direction in a low, deep drawl. Levander stared fixedly ahead as the taxi slid through the night. So distracted, so far away.

Millie half expected him to drop her off where she lived and carry on, but as the taxi slid to a halt outside the fabulous five-star hotel that Levander called home Millie almost wept with relief. He offered her his hand to step out, and they stood outside the grand reception area. A doorman opened the door for them and they stood in the blazing lights, watching the busy theatre of the hotel even at this impossible hour—a gaggle of women spilling out of another taxi, clipping their way across the marble, an airline captain dressed smartly in his uniform on his way to the airport—the same airport Millie would be at in a few hours…

'I'm sorry.' This time his apology was as unexpected as it was unnecessary. 'What happened back there…well, it is something I am used to. For you, though, I can see it would have been upsetting. Clearly it was a bad idea—'

'It was a lovely idea,' Millie broke in. 'And I actually had a lovely time—in fact, I think it's me that owes you an apology. I completely overreacted.'

'No,' Levander disputed, 'you did not. Sometimes I forget that not everyone has…' He hesitated for just a fraction too long, those beautiful eyes clouding over, and Millie frowned in concern.

'Not everyone has what?' she pushed, but he shook his head and forced a smile.

'It does not matter.'

Millie was sure that it *did* matter, but clearly he didn't want to talk about it. To help, she changed the subject. 'I still can't believe you actually live in a hotel.'

'Why not?' Levander asked. 'A few of their suites are for permanent residents.'

'But surely if your family are nearby…?' She gave a slightly helpless shrug. She didn't really know what she was asking—he was thirty, hardly likely to be living at home with his father, but it just seemed so temporary, so impersonal, so soulless. 'Does it really feel like home?'

'Sorry?' He stared back at her, a slight frown forming between his eyes as if he completely and utterly didn't understand her question, and Millie wondered if she'd spoken too fast—if perhaps he'd misunderstood something she'd said.

She rephrased her question, and spoke just a touch more slowly this time. 'Can a hotel really feel like a home?'

'Of course it feels like home.' He was still frowning down at her, as if surprised she'd asked such a strange thing. 'It is, after all, where I live.'

'I meant…' She gave in then—gave in not only because he didn't seem to grasp what she was saying, because whatever magic they had captured between them seemed to have evaporated. At least for Levander. The silence in the taxi, the terse responses to her questions, his apparent distraction, all pointed to one reluctant conclusion.

He'd had enough of her.

'I should go.'

'I know.'

'I really do have things I should do…' She was gabbling now, the words that had come so easily before now strained and forced as this most wonderful night came to a bitter conclusion. Levander, clearly bored with her company, was staring somewhere over her shoulder as she attempted to say goodbye.

Dared he?

It was a strange question for him to consider—for a man so used to women. It wasn't his seduction technique that was instilling such doubt—Levander knew she was ready. Despite the scene at the club, he'd felt her unfurl as he'd walked alongside her on the beach. What had happened between them in the café was what unsettled him. Hell, for a second there he'd lost all discretion—not just when he'd reached over and touched her, not just when he'd exposed her fragrant cleavage… She'd clouded his mind like a drug. He'd told her about the business, told her his thoughts. And for Levander that was unprecedented—so far removed from his usual reserve, at least where the family business was concerned, that it unsettled him. Disquiet seeped through his marrow at how this woman moved him so—how hard it was to field her questions. Because he actually wanted to tell her things, wanted to answer those perceptive questions…wanted her dizzy, happy perspective, wanted to lower his guard and laugh with her over and over again.

And if he kissed her he'd be lost.

'I have to go to the airport in…' She didn't have a watch, and as she looked at his and tried to read it upside down Levander relaxed.

She'd be gone soon.

Strange that it comforted him.

For a few hours he could hold her—concentrate solely on the one thing he did better than business, spend tonight with her, hush her questions with his mouth.

Indulge without consequence—safe in the knowledge that tomorrow she would be gone.

'…six hours.'

He was so tall she had to lift her head to look up at

him, but it was worth the effort, because finally he was looking at her—finally the Levander who had disappeared for a while had returned. And he was so exquisitely beautiful it was surprisingly easy to be bold, to lift her hand and touch his cheek rather than keep it by her side. She knew he was going to kiss her goodbye—could almost taste the lips that were moving in on hers—and she wanted it over and done with almost. Wanted to move away from this breathtaking man so she could remember how to breathe again, could get on with her life after this strange but dizzying pause.

Only she'd never been kissed like this before.

His mouth was incredibly soft on hers; for someone so masculine, he was surprisingly tender. His lips brushed hers, faint-makingly erotic, and her hands that had been on his cheek moved around to the back of his head. If a minute ago she had been conscious of the bellboy, the cars, the lights, now it all faded into insignificance. It was like being kissed for the first time—actually, way better than being kissed for the first time. His tongue stroking hers, his chin scratching her smooth skin, the intoxicating scent of him as he pulled her in closer, the feel of his hard taut body against hers. Nothing—not a case to be packed, nor a plane to be caught—got a look-in. Her whole being honed in on this delicious moment, and there was no question of wanting it to be over—just the knowledge that tonight it couldn't be.

'Six hours leaves no time for sleeping…' He pulled back just a fraction, his husky words not asking, but telling… Telling Millie what she already knew.

That the precious few hours she had left were for them.

It was as if all her rules had turned around—the inner compass that guided her running amok—north suddenly south—everything shifted.

This hadn't been a working holiday—it had been work, work, work. No sightseeing, no exploring this amazing country, and no romance.

Why, Millie begged of herself, why shouldn't she allow this one indulgence—this one crazy, impulsive moment with a man she'd remember for ever?

Remember for ever because, gazing into his eyes, Millie knew she could never forget—when everything else had crumbled, when all she had left were her memories, this would surely be one. The most beautiful, sensual of men holding her in his arms and wanting her.

He kissed her all the way up in the lift—and all the way back down to the foyer when they missed their stop. Urgent, hot kisses that were as fabulous as they were indecent. His impatient hand barely missed a beat as he hit the twentieth floor again, then returned to her bottom, cupping it, pressing it against him as his tongue worked its magic. He was kissing her mouth, her eyes, her ears, making her shiver. His body was pressing hers against the cold mirror, and his want for her was not remotely overwhelming—because it exactly matched hers. Desire was lacing its way through her body, the pressure against the dam that had been building for hours unleashing inside her the second he touched her.

Nerves only caught up as she entered his vast suite— her glittering eyes widening as she took in the opulent surroundings. She'd known he was wealthy, but it hadn't really equated till now. She felt her heels sink into the carpet and suddenly it unnerved her—standing in her cheap waitress uniform, every scrap of make-up thoroughly kissed away. She knew she didn't belong in his world. She was frozen with the awareness that she should be bathed and scented and gorgeous, and she was feeling anything but.

Levander didn't seem to notice at first, taking her in his arms and proceeding from where they'd left off. But then he sensed her unease.

'I'm sorry…' She felt like a tease, seeing utterly and completely the error of her ways, but she just couldn't *not* tell him. 'I don't belong here—this just isn't me…'

'What isn't you?'

'Here…' Millie wailed, her arms flailing, her breath coming out fast as she rued the ridiculous situation she'd found herself in. 'This isn't me…' And it wasn't just the luxurious surrounds that were panicking her, but Levander. Even after she'd seen the tears from Carla she had kissed him so fully, pressed her groin against his in the lift—she had taken, utterly and completely, leave of her senses.

'Levander, I'm not like this…like that.' She gestured to the closed door and the lift behind it, her cheeks scorching at the inappropriateness of it all. Shame was sweeping through her at the thought that in a few seconds she would have to clip her miserable way through the hotel foyer. She knew he couldn't possibly understand, and at first tensed, flinching, when he came over and held her. But her panic subsided a touch when she found that, actually, he did…

'*That* was not you…' His voice was low and soft in her ear as he held her trembling body. Her face was burning as she leant it against his chest. 'And *that* was not me,' Levander said, lifting her chin with his hands and forcing her to look at him. Her eyes stared in wonder and recognition as he continued. '*That*, Millie, was *us*.'

It made sense—for the first time in this mad night something actually made sense. It wasn't just about her or about him. It wasn't just Millie acting wildly out of character. It was about them—about the instant chemistry that had ignited, the longing, the want that had flared. *Such* longing.

She was shaking with arousal, literally trembling with want, and now that she understood it she could let it happen—could watch as his fingers opened the remaining buttons of her blouse, staring down at herself as if seeing her body for the first time, as if seeing it through his eyes, and actually feeling beautiful. He slid off her blouse, unhooked her bra, and all she felt was want—such want—as his tongue flicked her swollen nipple.

Such want as he slid the zipper down on her skirt till all she wore were her shoes and panties. His tongue traced a line down her stomach as he knelt ever lower, her thighs twitching with anticipation as he slid his way down…

'I should…' She hadn't washed, had been working all night, then walking the streets with him. But she didn't have to say it. Those dark eyes were looking up, meeting hers.

'It is you I want to taste—not soap, not perfume—it is your scent that has driven me crazy all night—don't take it from me now.'

He made it sound like a gift, like a treasure, his fingers parting the flimsy fabric of her knickers, then growing impatient, sliding them down over her bottom, her thighs. He buried his face in her damp bush, and Millie's last stabs of embarrassment were quashed by moans of pleasure. His tongue was like a cool, insistent pulse, and her fingers laced through his hair as her body both willed him to go on but begged him to stop. She was sure her knees would buckle as he worked on. Her pleasure was his, and she knew it—knew from his moans, from his hot breath and the tense fingers digging into her buttocks that Levander was as lost in the moment as she.

At that second it was imperative he was as naked as her, and he sensed it, pulling at his shirt. As he stood her impatient fingers wrestled with the belt on his trousers, and even though his lavish attention might have abated for a few seconds just the sight of him naked had Millie gasping—that gorgeous body, toned and delicious, merely a breath away.

He asked her.

As she stood there, eyes wide with lust, staring at him, he actually asked her what she was thinking.

She toyed with the idea of telling him the truth, tried to work out how to say what was truly was on her mind: that she'd never been with anyone before, that even though it must surely seem otherwise this was actually her first time—the first time she'd ever been this intimate with anyone. But she knew, just knew, she couldn't—knew from the little that she *did* know that the night would cease if she told him that truth. So instead she told him another—her answer raw and honest…

'It's beautiful…'

'Then hold it.'

So she did, tentative at first, and horribly, horribly gauche. But, feeling him so silken yet so strong beneath her fingers, something trilled inside her. Feeling him grow in her hand, feeling him harden beneath her fingers, wanton, reckless, yet terribly shy, she sank to her knees as she held him, her hungry eyes begging to please be allowed just a taste.

'Careful…' His throaty word was more a threat than a warning—his explosive device was so charged to the hilt that Millie knew that with one false move, with one hasty, gratuitous shift, it would all be over.

He was divine.

Greedy now, she devoured him—just so, *so* much pleasure in giving. She felt his fingers knotting in her hair, smelled the provocative scent of his most intimate place, felt black wiry curls kissing her eyes as she worked tenderly, boldly on…as he urged her deeper even while pulling her back.

'*Octahobka,*' Levander groaned, before repeating it in English. 'Cease now…'

There was no point trying to stand as he raised her up. Instead Millie fell on the vast bed with him—she so oiled and ready, and him so erect it was indecent. He was holding her—holding her so close she could hardly breathe—his lips kissing her eyes, his cheeks suffocating her with his desire. And it didn't matter about tomorrow; right now was enough. His tongue, hot and determined, pressed its weight on her, passion flaring as if they had been doused in petrol and set alight. His hands pushed her thighs apart more quickly than she could spread them. From his rapid breaths, from the rush of flesh swelling dangerously close, all she could do was guide him—guide him to her sweet, waiting entrance.

Her mouth was so full of his that she couldn't even call out as he thrust himself in, as her body adapted to the fabulous sensation of him inside her. It could have, should been over then. Only it wasn't. As if somehow just being there together was too good to end, his body sliding over and over hers, each measured stroke building towards a nearing target. Her throat, her stomach, her thighs contracted as still he bucked within, her fingers digging into his taut buttocks, her groin arching into his. She was weeping, frenzied, as he filled her, her orgasm so intense that she begged relief. But still he was bucking, still aroused when surely he should gladly wilt.

'I can't,' she wept in her exhaustion, 'Levander, I ca—'

Her sob was muffled by the muscle of his shoulder, and she bit into his salty flesh as she realised that, actually, she could.

'Millie.' He was pounding every one of her senses as he swelled further inside her, and though she had nothing to base it on, no touchstone to measure by, somehow as he eked the last dregs of restraint from her, as Levander spilled his full cup, taking her to the brink of insanity, she knew this was once in a lifetime. That this wasn't what she had been missing out on—this was what she must now forever miss.

And later, when exhausted, sated, she fell asleep beside him, instead of relaxing, instead of merely enjoying the precious time that remained, Levander wrestled with the impossible.

One heady taste had him hungry for more.

And not just for her body, but for her mind. He wanted those blue eyes to open on him—wanted to hear that voice—wanted more of the closeness they had shared tonight…

And that was what terrified him the most.

CHAPTER THREE

'YOU don't have to go.'

Waking to those words, Millie felt her heart still in her chest—her mind struggled to wake up, to assimilate all that had happened, and frantically she sat up, panic seizing her as she realised she'd fallen asleep.

Levander pushed her gently back down. 'It is only eight a.m. Relax.'

'Relax!' Millie let out an incredulous gurgle of laughter. 'I have to be at the airport to check in in two hours.'

'I say you don't.' He was propped on one elbow, leaning over her at the same time, his free hand stroking the outside of her thigh under the sheet, and for the second time in less than a minute Millie's heart stilled.

All the promise she hadn't dared glimpse dazzled her now, as she took in his raw naked beauty, that colourless face even more sensual somehow, his face pale in the stark morning sunlight, heavy-lidded eyes squinting slightly as he stared down at her—unshaven, untamed, and utterly unattainable, Millie decided with a reluctant sigh. Levander Kolovsky was so far out of her league it wasn't even worth considering the possibility. Last night had been amazing, undoubtedly the most romantic, sensual night of her life—and one she would never regret—but whatever magic had caused their stars to collide was one cosmic miracle that surely couldn't be sustained. They came from different worlds—and not just geographically. It had been too much, too soon, but completely unregrettable, and that gave her the courage to answer him honestly.

'Yes, Levander…' She watched as his eyes crinkled into a frown and then elaborated. 'I do.'

'If your visa is a problem then I can have my lawyer sort it out,' Levander said dismissively. 'Surely a few days won't make a difference? I can buy you another plane ticket if you have trouble cancelling at such short notice.'

His answer only strengthened her resolve—people like Levander gave no more thought to an international flight than Millie would to catching a bus, yet her airline ticket—the entire trip, in fact, had taken months of saving and planning. But, aside from that, a few more days wasn't going to change the ending to this dream. A few more days could only make the inevitable parting all the harder—at least for Millie.

'My family's expecting me.'

'Tell them you've been unexpectedly delayed…' His hand was moving to the inside of her thigh now, delivering long strokes, and though his touch was softer now the effect was heightened, making arguing her case all the more difficult. 'Tell them something came up…' His sensual mouth curled into a slow smile as he moved her hand to his morning erection. 'See—you would be telling the truth… You know it is too soon for this to end.'

He whispered the words to her left breast, taking the nipple in his mouth and sucking slowly, drawing sense from her mind with each decadent motion. His impact on her actually unnerved her, and if he touched her for even a second longer then Millie knew she was lost.

'No—I have to go, Levander…' Jerking her hand away, wriggling herself free from him, she stepped out of the warm bed, her words, her actions coming more harshly than intended.

She tried to read his expression, but it was as if bandit screens had come up at a bank—like looking at him, talking to him, through thick glass as he stood up and pulled on a robe. All the closeness, all they had shared last night, was gone now—and she couldn't blame him for what he must be thinking: that scenes like this for Millie must be the norm. They certainly were for *him,* she thought, remembering the beautiful teary Latina of the night before. Holding on to that thought, she squared her shoulders, grabbing her clothes and almost running for the bathroom, desperate for distance.

Closing the door, she sat naked and trembling on the edge of the vast bath. It *had* to be this way, Millie assured herself. For a dangerous moment she'd actually considered what he was offering—succumbing to his lovemaking, staying on for the golden few days he was offering. Peeling herself out of his embrace had taken a supreme effort, but the thought of ringing her family—

her family who, so excited at her return, were preparing a little welcome home party—telling them…

Telling them what?

Turning on the shower, Millie stepped in, closing her eyes as a blast of hot water brought her to her senses. That she'd met some rich guy a few hours ago who'd offered to buy her a new ticket? That she'd fallen into bed with a man she barely knew and was seriously considering letting everyone down just so she could get to know him a little better.

Millie barely looked at guys, was always so careful not to let anything interfere with her dream. And she had been, Millie realised. All her life she'd been careful—right up till this point. Her hand stilled on her body. In fact for a second everything stilled. And Millie wasn't sure if it was the water running or the blood gushing through her ears as an appalling truth hit.

Not only *hadn't* she been careful, last night she had been downright reckless. He was so intriguing, so intoxicating, so potently sexual she hadn't even considered contraception—hadn't thought of a single consequence.

Oh, God.

With a whimper of horror she almost doubled up in self-loathing.

Where had careful been when she'd needed it most?

Naïve, reckless stupid… Brutal words slapped her ears as she quickly dressed.

'Would you like some breakfast?' His voice sounded incredibly forced as she came out of the bathroom, and Millie couldn't really blame him. She was having trouble with her own words.

'I really ought to get moving.' She attempted a smile, but it faded when he didn't return it. 'Look, it really was terribly nice of you to offer to get me another ticket—'

'It probably is for the best that you go,' he interrupted abruptly. 'I am extremely busy over the next few days—I probably wouldn't be able to schedule much time with you.' Even allowing for his slightly limited English, his words were brutal. 'I'll make sure there is a driver available for you this morning—he can take you to your hotel, and when you are ready to the airport.'

And if it seemed like a kind offer, it only served to make her feel worse, if that were possible—as if somehow he were paying her back for her time. Perhaps the driver would stop *en route* and let her pick a bauble? She hated how he'd changed since she'd insisted that she was leaving—as if now he didn't even have to pretend to be nice to her any more. Tears glittered in her eyes as she declined his offer.

'I'd rather take a taxi.'

'As you prefer.'

She didn't bother with make-up. Rummaging through her bag, she just gave her hair a quick comb, wishing she could look more seductive, just a touch more fabulous as this amazing chapter of her life came to its sad close. But she couldn't. Couldn't just walk out on him as if last night didn't matter, and she couldn't tell him either just how much it *had*. So, awkward and horribly shy, but trying not show it, Millie tested the water.

'I can give you my phone number…perhaps you could give me a call?' It was a brave thing to offer, but incredibly stupid to lay herself so open to rejection, and it stung like hell when he shook his head.

'Perhaps not.'

Trying not to cry, trying to get out of his apartment with just a teensy shred of dignity, Millie didn't turn around. But she stilled for just a second as she walked out of the door and his beautiful rich voice delivered the strangest of farewells.

'You know where I am if you decide to come and get me.'

It took no time to get ready—three months of clothes thrown into a suitcase, her passport and tickets collected from the hotel safe and her bill paid. And as Millie took her second taxi ride of the morning, she stared at the streets she'd walked last night with Levander. She was filled with longing—almost homesick for a city she'd barely graced—and, passing the gallery, it was impossible not to stop for one last look. With the meter running she dashed out, blinking in amazement at the red dot on her painting. She raced inside and greeted an equally delighted Anton.

'You just had your first sale, honey.'

'Levander?' It was the only name on her mind, the only thing in her head. But the bubble of hope burst when Anton laughed and shook his head.

'I wish! No—some rather staid lady. You just missed her—the ink's barely dry on her cheque. Is there any way you can change your flight, Millie? Things could be turning around for you…'

She actually had a legitimate excuse to ring home

with now—a real reason to stay on just a little bit longer. But Millie couldn't do it. She wanted home, wanted her mum—and, Millie realised with shame, needed to see a doctor. She could still see Levander shaking his head when she'd offered him not just her phone number but the chance to get to know her a little better—a chance to somehow build on the one night they had shared. A few days as his *scheduled* plaything was the last thing she either wanted or needed to be.

'I really need to get back.'

'Shame.' Anton smiled. 'You should be sipping champagne with your gorgeous date from last night, not fleeing the country, you know. How on earth did you land him, Millie? Have you any idea how many women would kill for a chance to date him?'

'Does he date lots…?' Mille gulped. 'I mean, I gather he's no angel, but…'

'He's incorrigible.' Anton giggled. 'He'd only just started working at his father's company when he dated some actress—not that anyone knew who he was then. She was over here from the States to promote a film, and the next thing she was crying her eyes out on live television mid-interview because she'd just been dumped by Levander Kolovsky. Well, from that moment on the press have been in love with him, and his little black book reads like a Who's Who. We all live in hope that soon enough he'll work his way through the women and cross to the other side. We call him Georgie!'

'Georgie?'

'He kisses the girls, then makes them cry. It's probably best that you are leaving, honey. He'd soon mess up that pretty little head of yours.'

He already had.

As she climbed back into the taxi to head towards the airport Millie tried to fathom how in so little time so much could have changed. Selling her paintings had been her sole focus—everything had been geared towards making that first sale—only right now it barely seemed to matter. Everything that she had once deemed vital had gone tumbling to the bottom of her priorities. She barely knew him—and yet she felt different. As if in the couple of hours or so that she'd slept in his arms every molecule, every cell of her being had been taken out and then put back, only in a slightly different order.

'Could you go down Collins Street?'

The taxi driver just nodded. He probably didn't care if it took the whole day to get to the airport as long as the meter was running. But it was the most dangerous diversion of her life. As they approached the hotel, Millie asked him to slow down. She scanned the foyer for a glimpse, then stared up and up at the vast building, craning her neck. To see what, she didn't know—the thick black hotel windows gave no indication of what was going on inside. Truth be known, she had no idea which one was his. Yet she was sure, more sure than she'd ever been in her life, that Levander was staring down at her— that Levander was staring out through the window at her.

Watching her leave and maybe—Millie gulped—just maybe, waiting to see if she decided to return.

CHAPTER FOUR

'How could you let this happen, Levander?' Nina Kolovsky's voice was pure venom as she flounced uninvited into his office at 7 a.m. and slammed down a newspaper in front of him. 'All your father has done for you over the years—and here he is practically on his deathbed and you disgrace him this way.'

Usually it was Levander's favourite time of the day—he was always the first into work and more often than not the last to leave, and the couple of hours before everyone else invaded gave him a chance to focus without interruption. The sight of Nina at this hour, made-up to the hilt despite the supposed drama, was for Levander most unwelcome. Anyway, his father had been on his deathbed for four months now—and looking remarkably well on it. So well, in fact, that Levander didn't even bother to pick up the newspaper his stepmother was jabbing a well-manicured nail at. Couldn't be bothered to read about his supposed latest exploits, or read that the company shares had slid a quarter of one percent—just couldn't be bothered, full-stop.

'Out, Nina,' he drawled, his disinterest only inflaming her further. 'And I would prefer you arrange it with my secretary when you want to talk to me.'

'This won't wait!' Nina screeched. 'How could you do this to us? There is the reputation of our family to consider, your father's health. A shock like this could mean the end of him.'

Reputation.

It was the word he hated most to hear—a word that had been bandied around since he'd first set foot in Australia.

"Kolovskys has a reputation to uphold.'

"You will keep quiet, Levander.'

'You will be grateful for all your father has done for you.'

Not once.

Never.

His father and everything he was disgusted him—that he was a Kolovsky did nothing to make Levander proud.

'Annika pleaded with you to marry a nice girl, have babies—me, I pleaded with you to give your father his last wish, to let him go to his grave having seen the future of our family and the business. Instead you spit in all our faces—get some *cyka* pregnant—how could you let this happen?'

'You really think I am that stupid?' Levander sneered. 'As if I would be so careless, Nina. As if I don't know how many women would love to trap a man in my position. So, forget this rubbish you read…' He picked up the paper, ready to toss it in to the bin, ready to tell Nina to get the hell out of his office so that he could get on with his work. But his voice faded mid-sentence as he stared again at the eyes that had enchanted him, remembering the one time in his life he hadn't thought to be careful.

Because that night he hadn't thought—he'd felt.

'So you do know her, then?' Nina lit a cigarette and stood taking in his reaction, her face as hard as stone behind the make-up. 'You know this cheap, conniving tart—'

'Enough,' Levander roared, halting her filthy mouth momentarily. But the words hung in the air as he skim-read the article. Bile churned in his stomach as he read that not only was Millie pregnant, but that she'd deliberately withheld the information from him. Had chosen not to tell him—had even, Levander read, a great wave of nausea rolling over him as he did so, considered a termination.

'She would not do this.' It was a knee-jerk reaction, an absolute state of denial, because even though the paper screamed the words, the Millie he had met, *his* Millie, would never—could never say such things. 'She would not say these things…' Levander insisted, like a drowning man reaching for a safety rope—a man who would do anything to reach safe shores. He actually turned to Nina, sought comfort from the unlikeliest of sources, where he knew he would never receive the slightest of warmth. 'She would not do that.'

'Think with your head where this woman is concerned, Levander—because she has.'

'Meaning?'

'According to the paper your lady-friend's plane is due to land here in Australia in less than an hour.' Nina's grating voice jangled his every nerve. 'How convenient that this woman no one has ever heard of is suddenly in the news. She's made very sure there is no chance now of you paying her off quietly to get rid of her.'

'She's not like that.'

'Oh—and you know so much about her? Tell me, Levander—how did you meet this lovely girl?'

'That's none of your business.'

'It is *everyone's* business now,' Nina shouted. 'Read the rest, Levander. Read on and see that it says you met one night when you were out with your sister—she was waiting on your table. Given that you choose not to socialise often with your family—it narrows it down.'

'So?'

'You spoke in Russian or English?'

'What?' Levander frowned.

'That night—what language?'

'In English.' Levander frowned. 'Annika's Russian is not so good…'

'You fool…' Nina spat. 'Your little waitress tart heard every word—she knew you were upset, possibly that you were looking for a bride.'

'I wasn't upset,' Levander refuted. 'And if she had overheard she would have heard me tell Annika I most certainly am *not* looking for a bride.

'It is your father who is dying, Levander—even an insensitive brute like you would have felt something that night—and she knew it. That *suka* saw her chance and took it.'

'It wasn't like that,' Levander responded angrily. But Nina wasn't going to be silenced again.

'Tell me you were careful,' Nina demanded. 'Tell me you were careful that night and I will have PR straight on to it—Katina will have a retraction in tomorrow's paper and—'

'I'll deal with this,' Levander gritted.

'Tell me you were careful.' When Levander didn't answer, when he clearly couldn't tell her what she needed to hear, Nina sneered her disgust. 'You bloody fool!'

Levander closed his eyes, drew in his breath hard and held it, blocking out Nina's tirade and focusing only on Millie.

Pregnant.

Despite feeling as if a fist had been rammed into his stomach—despite his complete lack of preparation for the news—somehow it wasn't a complete surprise. Because a night like they'd shared couldn't ever just end, and for Levander it hadn't. Like trying to recall a dream, each morning he awoke to the fractured memory, chasing her image as it dispersed, trying to identify just what it was that had taken place that night, somehow assured that the energy they'd created couldn't just dissipate… No, it wasn't a complete surprise, Levander concluded.

That night had been too vast to amount to nothing.

'Where the hell's Katina?' As Nina grabbed for the phone, Levander caught her wrist.

'You already called her? You rang her before you spoke with me?'

'Of course.' Nina eyed him as if he were mad to think it an issue. 'She is our head of public relations…'

'Yours, perhaps, but she's not mine.' Picking up his briefcase, Levander marched to the door.

'Walk out, then,' Nina called. 'Walk out early on your contract while you're at it—walk out on your family when they need you most, when like it or not you need them too…'

'Need you?' Levander gave a mirthless laugh, didn't even look over his shoulder.

'How much time do you want to spend in your new job looking for a lawyer?'

'Take me to court,' Levander jeered. 'You think I've put up with you because I'm worried you'll sue, or because I don't think I can do better? I've put up with this because sadly you're family—because without me the House of Kolovsky would have been a joke by now.'

He was done.

Done with the lot of them. He couldn't even be bothered arguing the point with Nina—because he didn't care, hadn't for the longest time, and now it was time they got it. His only thought now was to get to Millie, to find out what the hell was going on.

'Why would we take you to court?' Nina's question went unanswered—striding across the office, Levander couldn't care less what she had to say. 'It's that little *cyka* who'll be taking you.' Keep walking, he told himself, don't even listen. 'To the family court, Levander…' He hesitated for less than a second, but that was all that was required for Nina to swoop. 'There it all comes out—there we sit in the gallery and watch others deal with our business. Ivan Kolovsky is dying, and his first-born son…'

Levander ran for an hour every morning—pounded the streets till it hurt and barely broke a sweat. But he was breaking one now… a sickly, cold sweat that came in seconds; he could literally feel the blood leach from his skin, feel the trip of his heart as it struggled to adjust to impending crisis. Rapid, shallow breaths dizzied rather than nourished, the blood rushing through his ears blocking her hateful words…his mind clamouring to find his own truth.

'And after that…' Nina's voice seemed to be coming from a great distance, pungent words that had the bile churning in his stomach. 'After everything has been said, when she's pulled our family and business apart and she's sitting laughing in England—then, Levander, *then* you will have to pay her.'

'I don't need Katina to deal with this….' He dragged the words out through pale lips.

'You might.'

'If I need her, I'll ask.' The world was coming back into focus now, but everything looked different—everything *was* different. He was stuck here, stuck here whether he wanted to be or not. Nina's bloated, over made-up face repulsed him so much he was sorely tempted to slap it, but he wouldn't give her a single second of martyrdom. Finding his voice, Levander said, more firmly, 'I'll sort it.'

'Sort it, then, Levander…' Nina jabbed a long red nail in his chest. 'And I tell you now, so you can tell that *suka* when you see her, whatever shame she brings to the Kolovsky table I serve her and her family double in return!'

'Levander…' Pale and distraught, Annika ran into the office, staring wide-eyed at him when she realised he clearly already knew. 'I heard it on the radio. You have to do something; the phones are ringing off the hook out there—the press are going crazy… Her plane's due to land soon—'

'When?' Levander cut in. 'When does her plane get in?'

'Levander,' Nina roared to his parting back. 'First we sort out properly what we do—'

'Get this.' He was back, his face just inches from Nina's, his face black as thunder as he eyeballed the woman he hated most in the world. 'I stay now because I have no choice. But you understand this—you are the *last* person I take advice from, the *last* person to tell me how I will raise my child…'

'Levander, stop it,' Annika sobbed. 'What are you saying? What are you doing? You know how sorry Papa is for what happened when you were younger, but that is done now—it cannot be changed.'

'Listen to your sister, Levander. We are all sorry for the past—' Nina started.

But this morning he could take it no more. Pandora's lid was lifting open and his rage bubbled to the surface. Because today—today Levander didn't want to hear those lies from Nina. Lies she repeated so often that sometimes Levander actually thought she must somehow believe them.

'You know it kills your father to think of what happened to you….'

'Don't even try, Nina,' Levander breathed, his voice low and menacing, speaking to her in Russian, watching as the colour seeped out of *her* face now. '*Min znatts.*'

I know the truth.

Finally—finally he was telling her the one thing she thought he didn't know, still speaking to her in Russian.

Just in case she remained in any doubt, he spelt it out just a little bit more. '*I remember what you choose to forget.*'

'Why are you speaking in Russian?' Annika's nervous voice had Nina's eyes darting.

'Ask your mother,' Levander said, without looking over, pinning Nina with his eyes, daring her to continue this conversation with Annika in the room, taking some small solace at the sheer horror on his stepmother's face. Now that she was finally silent, Levander had his say.

'Your mouth is filthy, Nina, and if I ever hear you speak of the mother of my child like that again then I will not be responsible for my actions. Oh—and I made a mistake before,' Levander said nastily, his accent heavy in his anger. 'It is my father who is the *last* person I take advice from—you, Nina, come a very poor second to last.'

CHAPTER FIVE

SELLING a painting, Millie mused, lifting up her tray and raising her seat as the cabin crew prepared for the final descent into Melbourne, was rather like having chicken pox—without the awful itching, though. One little dot had appeared, followed in rather quick succession by another two, and then little crops of them. A mention in the local newspaper had been followed by an interview with a national, then a couple of interviews on the radio. As her life's work had started disappearing around her, galleries who once hadn't even returned her calls had begun ringing to invite her to showcase her work—and, even though it was early days, any teaching plans had been happily deferred. And now here she was, revisiting Melbourne to personally deliver more of her work and to appear at one of Anton's swanky 'meet the artist' nights.

Though a rather flimsy reason to head halfway around the globe, it had proved enough of an incentive to muster all her courage and do what was becoming more and more unavoidable as each day passed.

Tell Levander.

His name popped into her head more times in a day than she dared to count. Working, shopping, eating, even while sleeping, he was a constant companion to her thoughts. Countless times she'd wanted to call him, to write to him, to tell him her news—but how could she?

God, she hated landing…the lights dimming in the cabin, no movie for distraction, the false hush that seemed to descend as her ears tried to adjust to the change in pressure, nowhere to go except to her thoughts…

She'd looked him up on the Internet.

The day she'd got home, before she'd checked her e-mails or waded through her post—almost as soon as politely able—she'd escaped to her computer and with a knot in her stomach she'd typed in his name. Expecting what, she didn't know. She had reeled as page after page, image after beautiful image, had mocked her a thousand times over. Masochistically almost she had forced herself to read interview after interview…though none directly with him. The occasional quote in the business papers was all she could find actually from Levander. Still, there were plenty of women happy to talk about him, and hardest of all for Millie to bear was that—unlike most women scorned—not a single one of them was vicious. Apparently Levander Kolovsky got a big red tick in every box. Their single pervasive complaint about Levander was merely that it was over.

How could she possibly tell him her news?

And how could she possibly not?

It was nearing winter in Melbourne now, and as the plane descended through the low, grey clouds Millie wondered for the millionth time what his reaction would be when she landed on his hotel doorstep.

Maybe she would ring up to his room and ask him to meet her in the bar. Maybe she should actually sit down and write the letter that was permanently penned in her head, give him a little time to digest the news before they had to face each other.

It was all she'd thought about for the last weeks and months, but especially now—walking through Arrivals—all Millie could think was that she was back in Levander's world, that soon she would see him. The thought was so consuming she had to ask the immigration officer to repeat his question as he flicked through her passport.

'I asked what is the reason for your visit?'

'Business,' Millie answered, frowning at his scrutiny and colouring just a touch as she realised she wasn't being entirely honest. 'Well, there are personal reasons too. But I am here for my work.'

'I'm more interested in those personal reasons.'

Immigration control was probably the only place on the planet where they could say such a thing and not get back a smart answer.

'I'm hoping to catch up with someone,' Millie croaked.

'A boyfriend?'

'Not really,' Millie said, flustered. 'He's just someone I met last time I was here—I'm hoping to see him, that's all.'

'Where will you be staying?'

'I've booked a hotel.' Millie tried to answer evenly, but her voice was growing more shrill. 'The same hotel I stayed in last time.'

'And you've no intention of staying longer than a month?'

'None…' Millie frowned, flummoxed by all the questions and for the first time worrying that she mightn't actually get in. 'Look, is there a problem?'

'That's what I'm trying to find out.' The officer gave a tight smile. 'Can I see your travel insurance documents?'

Blushing from her toenails to her roots, Millie handed them over, swallowing hard as he checked out the forms.

'I did check with my doctor that it was okay to fly while I was pregnant—I wasn't aware—'

'Have a nice stay!' Cutting her off mid-sentence, he stamped her passport, and Millie gave a tiny bemused shake of her head as she realised the mini-interrogation was over. It was almost as if he'd known she was pregnant and had been waiting for her to reveal it, Millie thought as she made her way over to baggage reclaim, and lugged her case and her carefully wrapped mountain of boxes onto her trolley. Oh, well, it was their job to be thorough.

Customs, in comparison to Immigration, was a breeze. Faithfully following the redline that meant she had 'something to declare,' Millie braced herself for a further barrage—but after a cursory look at her mountain of artwork and a brief look at her paperwork she was in.

'Welcome to Melbourne.'

'Thank you.'

'Would you like someone to escort you out, Miss Andrews?'

'I'll be fine.' Millie beamed, taken aback by the friend-liness and steering her massively overloaded trolley along the red line and out through the sliding doors.

For a second the flash of lights dazzled her—twenty-four hours on a plane and she was a touch dazed, to say the least, because at the end of the walkway was a group of photographers, all shouting out. For a second Millie faltered. Clearly she was blocking the path of someone rather famous. It entered her head to turn her trolley around and go the other way, but it was just too big and too overloaded to attempt the manoeuvre. Instead she glanced over her shoulder, ready to let whoever it was past. Somewhat puzzled, she took in the elderly couple dragging along behind her, and the frazzled mother with the even more frazzled toddler who had cried non-stop from Singapore: they didn't look particularly famous.

'Over here, Miss Andrews.'

'This way, Millie.'

It was *her* they were calling to. Mid-step, Millie literally froze, completely taken aback that these photographers were calling out to *her.* On closer inspection there were a few microphones amongst the crowds and a television camera. That a couple of radio interviews and a few lines in a newspaper could generate such interest just didn't add up. This was surely more the type of reception afforded Princess Mary than a struggling, almost known artist. Aware that her lank hair, her unmade-up face and, worse, her rather scruffy leggings and T-shirt, though comfortable for a flight, were pathetic to face the cameras with, for the second time Millie considered turning and running. What they hell did they want? Why were the press here?

And in that split second her question was answered.

It had little to do with her and everything to do with *him*.

Stepping out of the sidelines and into her line of vision was the man who had invaded her thoughts for sixteen weeks now…or one hundred and twelve days…or two thousand, six hundred and eighty-eight minutes. She knew that because she'd done the maths on the plane—only she'd never factored in *this*.

Dressed in a charcoal suit, his shirt so white Millie was tempted to scrabble in her bag for sunglasses, Levander actually surpassed the generous realms of her memories. He was, quite literally, breathtaking. Like some delicious Mafiosi movie figure who had stepped off the movie screen and into real life—her life—with that unruly dark hair neatly brushed back now, his dark morning shadow a mere memory because he was utterly, utterly clean-shaven. What was more, he was walking towards her as if he'd been waiting for her—walking towards her so purposefully that every atom in her body told her to run to him. She was the iron ore shavings in a school experiment; he was her magnet.

But as she let go of the trolley and in a reflex action went to run, something stopped her—something in his stance, his expression, telling her that even though he was holding his arms out to her, even though he was calling her name, for Levander there was nothing tender about this reunion. The thought was confirmed as menacing eyes held hers, his generous mouth taut and strained…

'Levander!' It was too confusing—too much to take in. Cameras flashed over his shoulder as her fellow travellers bumped their way past, the noisy buzz of a busy airport small fry to the whirl of questions spinning in her mind. 'What's going on?'

He didn't answer, just confused her more with his actions—dragging her fiercely into his embrace, clamping his mouth on hers so firmly that even breathing was impossible, kissing her so thoroughly, so passionately, holding her so tightly, that all resistance was smothered. He tasted just as divine as she remembered, felt as taut and as terrific as memory had told her. His scent was so intrinsically masculine, so replicate of her dreams, that it should have had her keeling over—*this* was the reunion she had secretly hoped for. If only his eyes weren't so cold…two black chips of ice staring down at her, belying the warmth of his embrace. And the hands seemingly holding her close were actually restraining her, holding her, kissing her, confusing her—until finally he drew back just enough to whisper into her ear.

'You, Millie, will say nothing—I will do the talking.'

'I don't know what…' Her voice was lost in the ferocious crowd. A man, presumably one of Levander's sidekicks, took her trolley as Levander walked her towards the waiting journalists. For all the world it looked like a protective arm around her, but it was more of a vice grip. She could feel the tension in his fingers as they dug into her shoulder. She was still reeling with shock as a microphone was thrust into her face, the sea of faces blurring as question after question hit.

'When is the baby due?'

'Do you have plans to settle here in Australia?'

'How long have you known?'

'When were you planning to tell Levander?'

Helpless, aghast, she looked up at Levander. The news she had wondered over and over how best to deliver was already public property. And the blows just kept coming—each revelation, each turn of events tumbling her further into confusion. Until Levander took control. Somehow, despite the slight grey tinge to his complexion, he appeared utterly unruffled, even the tiniest bit bored with the whole circus as he authoritatively addressed the hungry crowd.

'You will understand that my fiancée is tired after such a long journey.'

She opened her mouth to protest, to correct him, but his fingers tightened their grip around her waist—and thank God they did, Millie thought. Because otherwise her legs might have crumpled beneath her.

'Contrary to the scurrilous reports in your paper this morning...' Levander eyeballed one particular journalist, and Millie noticed the colour drain out of the poor woman's face as Levander continued with his response. 'We are both thrilled at the news that we are expecting a baby.'

'So you two *are* engaged?' Remembering her training, the journalist thrust a small tape recorder under Levander's nose.

'I believe that is what the word fiancée indicates.'

His sarcasm was biting—not that it stopped them. Microphones jostled for space as another burst of rapid fire hit, and Millie wanted to duck for cover, actually leaning into Levander as somehow, despite his loathing, he shielded her.

'What about your family?' a voice boomed above the rest, and the babble hushed as they awaited his answer.

'Delighted—naturally—and looking forward to the event.'

'Which is when?'

'Enough questions. My fiancée is clearly exhausted.'

And without another word he marched Millie out of the airport to a sleek black car waiting on the no-standing zone outside. Her luggage and her precious paintings were being loaded into the boot. When the driver opened the back door, for a second Millie wanted to turn and run—the photographers and the chaos in the arrivals lounge were infinitely preferable to facing Levander. Getting on a plane and heading for home even after a twenty-four-hour trip was way more appealing than getting into the car and facing him now. His anger was palpable as he snapped his orders to her.

'Get in.' Levander's words were like two pistol shots, and that once beautiful mouth was pale and taut as he spat the words out and took a seat. Only then did she realise how much she was shaking. While the driver finished loading her belongings into the boot they were alone for a few seconds, and she tried to regain control—tried to assert herself with this impossibly distant stranger.

'You had no right to say that I was your fiancée, Levander. No right at all.'

'No right?' He gave a low, mirthless laugh. 'You have no idea how many rights I have, Millie. And I intend to exercise each and every one of them.'

As the driver got into the car he leant closer towards her, and for a second she thought he was going to kiss her again, recoiling at the thought of another feigned show of affection. But the disgust in his eyes told her he felt the same, and his breath was hot with fury as his harsh whisper hit her ear.

'Some reading material for the journey,' he said, handing her a newspaper.

The bottom fell out of her world as she read the article, bile rising in her throat as she saw in print the hundred conversations that had taken place over the past few weeks with Janey, her friend. Private words, spoken in confidence as she'd struggled to come to terms with the fact she was pregnant, were all distilled into the most potent of poisons. Tiny fleeting thoughts that had entered her troubled head were neatly typed in black and white for the world to see, and worse—far worse—for Levander to read…

'Oh, God, Levander. I never—'

'Save it,' he hissed, calling for his driver to get going, then leaning back on the leather seat and reading over her shoulder as tears coursed down her cheeks. 'This bit's my personal favourite…' He jabbed his finger at a paragraph.

Millie couldn't have read it if she'd tried, her eyes were swimming with tears. But she knew without looking what he was referring to: that horrible night when she'd explored her options out loud, the fleeting moment when she'd examined the possibility of ending the pregnancy and getting on with the scattered fragments of her life. How cold, how emotionless it sounded as he read it aloud to her—how devoid of the desperation that had made her voice tremble as she'd sobbed the appalling thought to Janey. Though what trashy journalist worth his salt, what friend greedy for a quick dollar, would bother to add in the convulsive tears that had followed, to say that even before she'd finished talking she'd shaken her head in hopelessness, knowing for her it could never be an option?

But how could a man like Levander possibly understand?

'Maybe we should cut this out and save it for the first page of the baby album?' Back in his hotel room, still the onslaught continued, his contempt so palpable it was like being slapped.

'Don't say that,' Millie begged.

'Oh, but you were the one who *did*,' Levander threw back at her coldly.

'I know it must have been awful to find out like this—'

'You know nothing,' Levander sneered. 'Is this all true—what is written?'

'No…' Millie attempted, then gave a helpless shake of her head. 'Some if it. I did say some of it…'

'All of it, perhaps?' Levander interrupted. 'Don't lie to me here, Millie.'

'I'm not,' Millie gulped, still frantically looking for an out. 'Papers make up stuff—exaggerate things… Surely you of all people would know that?'

'They would not dare.' He halted her attempt, his voice curiously calm now. Only it did nothing to soothe her, each word he delivered backing her further into her miserable corner. 'This newspaper I have already sued— already forced to print a retraction when they were less than accurate with their reporting. Two years ago they accused me of sleeping with the wife of one of our rivals—the truth was we had met for lunch twice, as she was planning a surprise party for him. That surprise party nearly cost her her marriage. They have been waiting to get me ever since, and I know they would not go to print unless they could account for every word. So tell me, Millie, and I would appreciate the truth—did you or did you not consider withholding the news about the baby from me? Consider that you would just raise the baby without my knowing?'

She had—the night she had performed her pregnancy test, when her whole world had spun out of control, yes, she'd thought about it—about if she was actually pregnant never letting him know. But almost instantly she'd dismissed the idea, and now, sitting on his sofa, hearing the accusation in his voice was more than she could bear. 'I did—but I'm here, aren't I?'

Levander didn't respond, just hurled another question. 'And did you also consider terminating the pregnancy?'

Millie ran a dry tongue over her lips, a fresh batch of tears threatening. Her attempts to hold them back were rewarded with a running nose, and she gave a rather ungracious sniff before she finally answered, in the shakiest of voices, 'For about two minutes.'

The look of absolute disgust on his face told her exactly what he thought of her response.

'And while you were so—you will forgive me if I quote,' he checked nastily, picking up the hateful paper and reading loudly, each word like a hurtling knife aimed in her direction. 'While you were so "confused and vulnerable", it says that your friend Janey kindly pointed out to you that, given my extreme wealth, you and the baby would be well looked after, and that there were "plenty of women who would give their eye teeth for a regular maintenance cheque from a Kolovsky".'

'They were her words.' Millie shivered.

'But, "I'm here, aren't I?" were yours,' Levander cruelly pointed out. 'Here to arrange your regular cheque, Miss Andrews? Here to make sure that your future is secured?'

'I'm here to tell you that I don't know what to do…' The tears were coming now, and the fear, the misery, the utter bewilderment of the past sixteen weeks was nothing compared to the horror of facing Levander in this mood. 'I'm here to tell you that I've messed up our lives and that I'm having a baby.'

'Well, as you can see…' utterly unmoved, he stood there '…I already know.'

'I'm sorry.'

'Save it for later,' Levander sneered. 'Save it for our child when it learns how to read.'

'Stop it,' Millie sobbed, placing her hands over her ears, hysteria rising in her voice. 'Please, just stop it. I never meant for those things to be printed, and I never, *ever* want the baby to hear them.'

'Drop the drama, Millie, it does not move me.' His voice was eerily calm, but his face was menacing as he stepped in closer, his two hands removing hers from her ears and pushing them down by her sides, pinning her against the wall, not with his strength but his hatred. 'Tell me, have you cancelled your gym membership yet?'

'What?' She had no idea where he was going, her mind a blizzard of thoughts attempting to focus on his strange question.

'You told me that night you pay for your membership but you don't go…'

'So…?' Her eyes darted, looking for an out, looking at anything other than him—the wall preferable to the sheer loathing in his eyes.

'I find that lazy.'

'I don't understand…' Millie whimpered, feeling his hot breath on the shell of her ear, feeling the bristling emotion emanating from him, shivering with misery at all they had become. 'I don't understand what you're saying.'

'Then allow me to explain better. When I sign for something, when I pay for something, when I set my mind to something, I make the most of it—every time.'

'What does my gym membership have to do with this?' Millie asked. But she knew what was coming, and wanted to slam her hands over her ears again as he spat out his demands.

'I am telling you that I am not lazy, Millie. Don't think for a minute you get a cheque from me and I make an occasional visit.'

'I wasn't th—thinking that at all…' Her teeth were chattering so violently she could barely get the words out.

'Don't think I pay my membership and then forget, or I am too busy to come. I am there every time.' He was there now, right in her face as he made himself beyond clear, his accent more pronounced in his anger. 'Making use of all facilities, making sure I get full use—'

'No!' Millie shook her head at what he was surely implying, but Levander just laughed in her face. 'You think I talk about *you?* You think I could want you after reading this filth? I am talking about our baby—I am in that child's life now, whether you like it or not. So get used to seeing me, Millie. Get used to it quickly—because I am in your life now, every day.'

Emotion and exhaustion, coupled with a good dose of the morning sickness that had her feeling so wretched, so weak, washed over her. She couldn't even attempt to argue with him—to thrash out the details that she knew had to be sorted. She just wanted to close her eyes on the horror, to find somewhere safe where she could lick her wounds and regroup.

'We'll talk about this later…' Somehow she found her voice, somehow she managed to look at him, her red, bloodshot eyes trying and failing to recognise the man she'd thought she once knew. 'You do what you have to, Levander, and I'll do what I can. But right now I'm going to my hotel…'

'You're staying here.'

'After the way you've just spoken to me? You really think that I'm going to stand here and attempt to defend myself to you when you've clearly already made up your mind?'

'You have no choice,' Levander retorted. 'There are photographers, press down in the foyer. You really think they will just let this story go?'

'Why the hell are they so interested?' Millie flared. 'What does it have to do with them?'

'I am a *Kolovsky!*' Levander shouted at her for the

first time—and it was almost a relief. Raw anger was easier to face than the simmering hatred that had greeted her at the airport. 'I am one of the wealthiest single men in Australia—my *life* is their interest. Do not pretend for a single moment longer that you didn't know that. Now, if you choose to go down there and make matters worse instead of better then I will not stop you. I wish you luck getting past them and into a taxi. I wish you luck checking into another hotel and trying to get the sleep you clearly need…'

He had a point, Millie realised, recalling the frenzy of the press at the airport. The thought of facing them without Levander to control them wasn't particularly appealing.

'Go to bed.' He must have sensed her hesitate and he seized on it, his voice more reasonable now. 'Go to bed and I will not disturb you. Rest, and then, when we have both calmed down…'

'When did you find out?' For the first time she got to ask a question—strange the details that mattered when chaos reigned. 'Did they call you to confirm…?'

'I read it an hour ago.'

It took a moment for it to sink in, for her to realise how low the press had really stooped, the shock tactics they were prepared to use. She might have landed in Melbourne to face that greedy crowd alone. And even if Levander's greeting had been less than cordial, even if his words had been reprehensible, she was grateful that despite his own shock he'd been there for her.

'I was going to tell you.'

'Just go to bed, Millie.'

Only she couldn't now. The massive impact that had

hit was receding, but aftershocks were rippling in. 'I really thought she was my friend…' Rubbing her fingers on her temples, Millie struggled to take it all in. 'I trusted Janey. I can't believe—'

'It is done,' Levander interrupted. 'Now it is time to fix it.'

'Can we?'

'I will think of something,' Levander answered. 'When you go to bed I will speak with the public relations people and work something out. Tonight we will have dinner with my family. At least if we put on a united front for now…' His voice trailed off. Perhaps he was realising she was too dammed exhausted to take it all in, too bone-weary for out-loud musings. 'Get some sleep, Millie; just try not to think about it now.'

With a tired nod she headed to the bedroom, peeled off her clothes and sat on the edge of the bed in her bra and knickers, wondering just what the hell she should do— how on earth it had come to this, how she could possibly tell her parents what had happened since her arrival in Melbourne. She jolted as yet another aftershock hit.

'Oh, no…' A whimper of horror escaped her lips as the implications of the very public demise of her reputation became all too apparent—as the appalling realisation hit that her parents would probably already have read a similar article in the UK, would be reeling in horror at the thought of their daughter landing on the other side of the world to this nightmare.

They already knew.

Everyone knew.

That was why the immigration officer had given her

such a hard time. He had known she was pregnant—had known because he'd read about it…

'I need to borrow your phone…' Her tear-streaked face appeared at the door. She didn't even notice he was standing where she had left him, talking on his mobile.

'Of course.' He gave a bemused nod. 'Is the one by your bed not working?'

'It's an international call…' Mille started, then understood the confusion behind his question. The richest, most eligible bachelor in Australia clearly didn't give two hoots about his phone bill.

Perhaps he heard her numerous attempts, understood that in her emotional state the international code to the UK might not come easily to mind, because after a few moments he came in, dialled in the number, and turned to go. He halted as she literally crumpled at the sound of her mother's hysterical voice.

Seeing her standing in just a bra and knickers, shivering in her own misery, hearing her shaking voice begging her mother to calm down, for the first time he wasn't thinking about the baby, nor was it the vile words in the article that consumed him. For that moment it was her. Her pain, her anguish, was so raw, so deep, even Levander couldn't remain unmoved. He placed a hand on her shoulders for support as she doubled up with the pain of it all.

'Mum, please,' she begged, over and over. 'It's not that bad. I'm fine—the baby's fine. I know—I can't believe what's happened… You have to calm down. I can hear Austin getting upset. Please, Mum, it really isn't as bad as it seems…' But clearly Mrs Andrews didn't believe her daughter; Levander could hear her cries as Millie attempted to reassure her.

'I don't know why Janey did it either. She's been acting a bit strange recently—I thought she was a bit jealous about my paintings. But whatever her reasons, it's done now…'

Again his conviction wavered. The anger, shame and humiliation at being the last to know, the sheer panic that had propelled him to the airport, dimmed a touch as he started to see things from Millie's side.

Her best friend had betrayed her. Her whole life was under the microscope. Though for him it was the wretched norm, for Millie it must be like awaking to a nightmare. Seeing her pale, shellshocked face, listening to her try to sound upbeat for the sake of her mother, he felt something inside him shift—and not just towards her. Guilt flickered in for the way he had spoken to her, for the anger he had unleashed towards the mother of his child.

His child.

The realisation was starting to hit home. She was carrying a baby—his baby—and the thought literally paralysed him, terrified him more than Millie or anyone could ever know. Yet somewhere deep within there was a flicker of excitement—a flare of want for the tiny life they had created.

A strange defensiveness towards her.

'Do you want me to speak with your mother?' Levander offered. The sudden change in his manner obviously confused her, and he watched as Millie's stunned eyes jerked to his. Though she shook her head, and gripped the phone tighter to her, he could tell she was considering it. 'I will tell her that I am sorting things out.'

'I don't think speaking to you will help right now…' Mille covered the mouthpiece with her hand. 'But I don't know what else to say. She's really upsetting my brother. I just can't calm her down.'

'I will talk with her,' he said, and even though he had no idea what he should say, he *was* ready to step in. But as he held out his hand Millie shook her head, closing her eyes as she swallowed her bitter medicine—the united front she'd so vehemently opposed just a few moments earlier was the only viable option for now at least.

'Levander met me at the airport, Mum…' She blew her hair skywards as her mother's hysterics halted. 'He's dealing with the press. I promise you he's taking care of it, and that things will all seem better tomorrow. I'm at his home, he's standing next to me now…' She was trying to sound positive—happy, even.

But seeing the tears coursing down her cheeks as she spoke, as she tried to look out for her mother, made Levander feel like an utter heel.

'Honestly, Mum—Levander's not cross. He knows me better than to take what Janey said at face value. We're going out tonight with his family. Yes…' With her free hand she pushed his off her shoulder, gritting her teeth as she lied into the phone, her eyes blazing with loathing for Levander as she spoke. 'Please don't worry—tell Dad not to either—everything's going to be fine.'

Finally, when nothing she could say would appease her mother, when she could hear Austin's mounting distress in the background, Millie gave in, handing the phone to Levander and dropping to the bed, hugging her knees and biting on her lip, wondering what reaction he would get.

'Mrs Andrews, I am sorry we have to first speak in these circumstances. I understand that you must be distraught, but let me assure you that your daughter is okay…'

He was so commanding, so perfectly polite and yet so effortlessly charming, that the tears, the panic that was engulfing her stilled. Millie jerked her head upwards as clearly Levander had the same effect on her mother. The buzz of anxious chatter spilling out of the phone hushed as Levander took control—but even as he said the right things, even as he soothed with his silken voice, still he unnerved her. Like a doctor walking in and giving a cancer diagnosis, his delivery was slick and effective, riddled with fact yet utterly devoid of compassion.

'I met her myself at the airport, and I will tell you now what I told the press, so you get no more surprises—I have asked that your daughter be my wife. Tonight we are going out with my family to make things official.' He handed the receiver back to her and Millie listened to her much calmer mother, twittering away, saying that Levander sounded nice, that it sounded as if he had things under control, was she sure she was really okay…?

'Honestly, Mum, I'm fine.'

Millie dropped the receiver into the cradle, and her voice was a monotone when next she spoke, her eyes dull when finally she managed to look at him. 'Well, you got what you wanted—you got your united front.'

'I always get what I want,' Levander said ominously. 'Always.'

* * *

She could go.

Sitting in semi-darkness, all phones turned off finally Levander could think. He had had to resort to calling hotel security and insisting someone be placed on his floor, to halt the endless banging on the door, telling them that under no circumstances, no matter how dire the emergency, was he to be disturbed.

This was the emergency he must deal with.

What the hell had he been thinking? Over and over he berated himself for even thinking of taking her out to dinner tonight—exposing her to the snake pit of his family and the chance of stumbling on the truth.

He managed a glimmer of a smile as he envisioned her happy, lively voice attempting conversation, asking questions that, when you were with a Kolovsky, were completely out of bounds.

They'd crush her.

He had to somehow warn her without telling her—but how?

How many times he'd headed to the bedroom door, braced himself to enter, to wake her from her much needed slumber and tell her what was on his mind, Levander didn't know. A couple of times he had even got as far as opening the door, standing for a breathless second or two and watching her sleep—her tumble of curls sprawled across the pillow, the steady rise and fall of her chest, long eyelashes fanning her cheeks and the flicker of her eyelids that told him she was dreaming…

How could he wake her to tell her his nightmare?

And if he did, then what?

How could Millie, how could anyone, fathom what he

was feeling? And anyway, if he told her his truth—if he exposed his family secret—she could use it against him. Closing his eyes, Levander dragged in air, his mind racing faster—wincing at the prospect of the Kolovskys undertaking damage control. Like a flawed piece of silk, she'd be relegated as seconds, her name muddied and soiled till there was nothing of her left—anything was permissible if it meant preserving the family's reputation.

He stared at the passport sticking out of her handbag, sitting beside the suitcase half opened on the floor beside the bed. He figured at most it would take her five seconds to pack and walk out the door.

And who could blame her?

He couldn't keep her a prisoner here. And no matter how loudly he might have insisted today that he would fight her all the way, a woman like Millie wouldn't take long to regroup—in a day or two the wind would be back in those glorious sails and she'd be gone.

They'd be gone.

On the next flight to London, with all the ammunition she needed to fight her case. What court in what land would rule in his favour?

Nina's jeers were coming back to haunt him now… making him imagine the vile outcome if Millie ever had her day in court.

It wasn't the fear of losing money or reputation that had stopped him in his tracks with Nina—it was fear of the court's inevitable decision that had chilled him to the bone.

How could she *not* be the better parent?

Closing the door behind him, Levander knew what he had to do.

Stepping into his lounge, he pulled back the curtains and stared out at the wintry morning, at the heavy grey clouds that smothered the skies Millie had been in so recently—the skies that would surely claim her if somehow he didn't get in first.

She had to marry him.

His breath whistled through his teeth as he let it out.

He couldn't let his guard down for a second—couldn't let her even a tiny bit close till that ring was safely on her finger.

Whether she wanted to or not, Millie had to marry him so he could protect them all.

CHAPTER SIX

'MILLIE?' Jumping at his rather brusque greeting, blinking as the bedroom door opened, Millie could only compare this awakening to her father coming in a decade earlier, when she'd stayed out too late and partied just a little harder than she'd promised her parents she would.

'Am I grounded?'

'What?' Cruelly turning on the lights, he frowned down at her and placed a heavy glass of water on the bedside table. Despite not wanting to accept anything from him, the chink of ice against the glass, combined with a very dry mouth, had Millie reaching over and gulping thirstily as Levander continued. 'It is time for you to get ready. I tried to let you sleep as long as possible, but our dinner reservation is for eight.'

'Oooh…' Millie closed her eyes and leant back on the pillow. 'How could I forget that little gem?'

'You should start to get ready.'

'Do we really have to go?'

'We agreed on it.'

'Actually, no, *we* didn't.' Sitting up, Millie wrapped

the sheet around her, her woolly jet-lagged brain functioning a lot better after a decent sleep. 'I was told there were a lot of things I ought to do, but I can't actually remember agreeing to any of them. And for your information I don't want to go—so I'm not.'

There. With a little nod at the end, she said it and, closing her eyes, rested back on the pillow.

'Are you always this selfish?' She'd expected him to stalk out—had prepared herself for a rather loud slam of the door—but instead he stood over her. Not that she could see him—her eyes were still firmly closed—rather she could feel his brooding presence, hear the contempt in his voice as he stared down at her. 'You really think *I* want to do this tonight? You really think *I* want to be out with my family, posing for happy-family shots after all that has happened?'

'Then don't,' Millie attempted, only her voice wasn't quite so brave. Peeking one eye open, she remained insistent.

'We have to make things better.'

'How?' Millie demanded. 'How could it possibly make things better? Frankly, from where I'm standing—or rather lying—going out tonight hand in hand, and pretending everything is okay between us, can only make things a whole lot worse.'

'Ring your mother and tell her that, then.'

'Fine.'

'And then you can ring the restaurant and tell them to cancel the booking, and let our guests know when they arrive.'

'They're *your* family,' Millie said, huffing onto her

side—hating what they had become, refusing to be forced into a corner.

But the sight of her back didn't halt him. In fact it inflamed him. 'And they are the very last people I want to dine with—who, despite what you read, I do not get on with.'

'So why—?'

'Why?' His voice was incredulous. 'You have the temerity to ask *why?* Do you ever stop to think of consequences, Millie? Do you ever think more than five minutes ahead in your life?'

'Of course…' she attempted.

'You know…' He shook his head in disbelief at her response, and with each passing word his accent was more pronounced. 'My family think you trapped me—they try to tell me you *knew* what you were doing that night—'

'I didn't.'

'I know that,' he roared. 'Despite what everyone says, I *know* that—because I think you're too dizzy to even come up with it…because you just don't think, do you? You meet a stranger, forget your pill…'

'It takes two…' Millie shivered.

'One night, *trajat'sya,* of sex, and now we pay the price—now we do as countless other couples have done when their one night of lust comes back to haunt them.'

'Haunt them!' Millie gasped. 'Levander. How could you say such a thing…?'

'How could I not?' Levander barked. 'What did you think would happen here? Did you expect me to start crying? To take you in my arms and say this is the best news I could imagine?'

'Of course not.' Unwanted tears welled in her eyes. His choice of words was so appalling, she simply couldn't help herself—the fact that he saw this baby like some dark ghost coming to haunt him was almost more than she could stand.

'So what did you think, Millie? Come on—tell me—what-did-you-think-was-going-to-happen?' Her threatened tears didn't move him. 'You don't *think* when you walk out on me, when you don't bother to tell me about our baby, of the consequences. Instead you open your mouth to your so-called friend. Well, unlike you, I *do* stop to think—I think of ten, fifteen years from now, when our child can read, when it stumbles on the filth that you spouted.'

'It won't be like that—'

She didn't get a chance to finish. Two strong hands were ripping at the sheet, pulling at it like a magician with a tablecloth—only instead of plates and cutlery left intact on the table it was a thoroughly shaken Millie left lying on the bed as Levander stood over her.

'This is not about what *you* want and it is not about me. It is about our child.' He didn't point, he didn't even look, but exposing her, letting her glimpse the full horror of a future without first making amends somehow made his words sink into her core. 'That newspaper article will always be there, the slur getting bigger with each passing day unless we halt it right now. Tonight we can make it right—make sure that when our child is old enough to stumble on it, be horrified by it, he or she will find out that the next day it was all discounted. So get up, get dressed, and get smiling—tonight we do our best for our child's future.'

Which didn't exactly give her much choice.

Pale, shaking, and feeling utterly wretched, she climbed out of bed. Though he was loathsome, he was also right—and she could actually glimpse an exit from the impossible, unsalvageable situation Janey had dumped them in. She even managed a wry smile as she glanced down at her suitcase. Which reminded her of her next problem.

'I know in theory it shouldn't matter a jot...' Jet-lagged, and as dizzy as if she'd drunk half a bottle of champagne, Millie raked a hand through very messy hair as she rummaged through the case. She was talking to herself more than him, delivering a swift pep talk and pulling funny little faces as she did so. 'I should just be myself, and not care about the cameras or the fact I'm dining with the *Kolovskys*...'

She pulled out the faithful red dress that had seen her through a couple of weddings, many first and last dates, and hopefully—if she didn't put on another ounce between now and next Friday—would see her through the 'meet the artist' night. Millie groaned at the blob of dessert she'd meant to dry-clean to oblivion, and closed her eyes in hopelessness. Resting back on her heels to look up at Levander, she missed the glimmer of a smile that briefly dusted his lips.

'Levander—what the hell am I going to wear?'

She sighed in utter relief when he delivered his answer. 'It is all taken care of.'

It was.

He must have had the entire Kolovsky range transported to his suite, and a hairdresser and a make-up artist were awaiting summons. Weary, utterly drained, and still stinging from his words, for now she played along with Levander's spin doctors, hoping and praying that even if Janey's words couldn't be erased, somehow they might manage to dilute them.

Choosing from such a dazzling selection of evening wear was a feat in itself, though. The stunning colours and heavy silks that were such a trademark of the Kolovsky line, though undoubtedly fabulous, were just a touch too vibrant for five feet three of drooping exhaustion. Even the basic black seemed just a touch too opulent. But there, amidst them, was the palest grey dress, its silk so thick it felt like wool, and as she slid it over her head for the first time Millie could see why people spent thousands to own a dress as fabulous as this. The cut of the fabric was to die for, tapering over her ribs, and there was soft ruching over her stomach which took away any attention from there and diverted it to her bust—the empress neck somehow giving Millie's rapidly expanding cleavage absolute centre stage.

With a cape draped around her she closed her eyes as the hairdresser transformed her strawberry-blonde curls into a thick glossy mass while the make-up artist, with as much skill with a brush as Millie herself possessed, accentuated her blue eyes with grey eyeshadow, lashings of mascara, and made her lips so full and sexy it was a shame she didn't feel like smiling.

'That's better.' Levander barely even glanced in her direction as he lifted his collar and fed in a tie. 'We'd better get moving.'

'Am I allowed to ask who's going to be there?'

'My father Ivan, his wife—my stepmother—Nina, and no doubt her ugly sisters and their hangers-on. And my half-sister Annika will be there, too.'

'The one I saw you with at the restaurant?' Millie asked, and Levander nodded. 'What's she like?'

'Sweet.' Levander shrugged, then cursed as his tie refused to knot. '*Govno.*'

Watching him heading to the mirror, muttering under his breath and knotting his tie there, for the first time Millie actually registered that he was nervous.

'And that's it?'

'That is enough for tonight. I have two half-brothers—twins, Aleksi and Iosef—but they are overseas. Aleksi is in London, working for the company.'

'And the other twin?' Millie asked, overwhelmed and wretched at the impossibility of them all.

'Iosef is a doctor—a trauma specialist,' Levander clipped. 'He has been working in Russia for the last five years.'

Which sounded rather more safe and normal—strange how the most esteemed profession could sound positively bland when you were a Kolovsky.

Tie still nowhere near knotted, he glanced over to her. 'Here.' Digging in his pocket, he pulled out a ring—with no box or bow, and absolutely no ceremony. 'You'd better put this on.'

'Dig myself in deeper, you mean?' Millie retorted.

'Don't play the innocent. I told your family and mine that tonight we will make things official—we can hardly do that without a ring.'

Pushing the ring on the suitable finger, Millie gave it less than one glance and certainly not a second. She wouldn't give him the bloody satisfaction. 'Well, so long as you know I'm a firm believer in long engagements. I'm not going to be pushed into anything.'

'And as long as *you* know that I'm not to be pushed *out* of anything either—then at least we'll understand each other. You'd better help me with this. I can't get it to sit right.'

He *was* nervous, Millie thought again, fiddling with his tie knot. And so was she—and not only about tonight. Standing less than a few inches away from him, trying to sort out the mess he'd made of his tie, she could feel his body was rigid with tension. His eyes stared fixedly ahead, and he was so tall her face was at his chest—so close it was impossible not to breathe him in, not to notice the strong angle of his fresh-shaven jaw, the thick set of his neck, impossible not to think of the last time they'd been this close.

What did this man do to her?

Her hands were shaking like an addict, her body craving the next dangerous fix. She focused on the ring she'd sworn not to pay any attention to—but a generous carat of diamond was a poor diversion when it was attached to a hand that was touching him.

'That's better…' She had to clear her throat to speak, and stepped back a bit, admiring a little more than her handiwork. 'Should we go?'

'We're supposed to wait for Katina.' Levander glanced at his watch. 'She is our head of PR—she should be here by now to brief us.'

'Brief us?' Millie gave a nervous giggle. 'We're going for dinner with your family. How bad can it possibly be?'

'No worse than today…' He gave her the coldest of smiles. 'Unless, of course, we find out tomorrow that you chatted to someone else—got bored on the plane, perhaps, and discussed—'

'That's uncalled for—Janey was my friend…I trusted her.'

'So who's the fool?' Levander sneered. 'Who has to clean up the mess now? You know…' he actually deigned to look at her '…I cannot make out if you just pretend to be stupid or if you really are.'

'You bastard.'

'Correct.' Livid, he faced her. '*I am* a bastard. I grew up a bastard. And if you think for a second I will allow my child the same fate—then you really are beyond stupid. I'm tired of waiting for Katina. Let's get this over with.'

He had the nerve to offer her his hand as they went out through the door, but reeling, stunned and terribly close to tears, she shook her head, pulling her bag tight over her shoulder. And even though he was beside her as she stepped in the lift, as she remembered their first night in there, all the love and emotion that had somehow jetted them to this bitter point, she could hardly bear it—she couldn't keep the truth from him for even a second longer.

'What you said…' Millie attempted. He was pushing the button, the lift doors were sliding downwards. Soon they'd be hurtled out into the public, to his family, and suddenly it was imperative that he knew the truth. 'I didn't forget.'

'Leave it now.' As the lift plummeted Levander frowned over, but she couldn't.

'I didn't forget to take my pill.' She watched his face tauten. 'I didn't forget because I wasn't even on the pill.'

'Are you telling me that Nina was right? That you knew exactly what you were doing?'

The lift stopping on the twelfth floor prevented further discussion. An elderly couple stepped in—dressed to the hilt and utterly gorgeous, they made polite greetings, then held hands as the lift plummeted again. Their obvious love and affection for each other was a bitter contrast to Levander and Millie. When they finally arrived at the ground floor they were greeted by a pretty little thing, no doubt hand-picked by Levander, stepping forward and smiling brightly, introducing herself as the Kolovsky head of PR.

'You were supposed to wait for me, Levander.'

'You were late,' he answered tartly.

'Nina took a little longer than expected. Now—no interviews, no comments, no matter how provoked, and above all else make sure they can see the ring.'

Pretty and smiling she might be, but she was as sharp as a tack, her shrewd eyes taking in the pair of them.

'Get over it now, guys,' she hissed through her glossy red lipstick. 'The photographers are mainly at the restaurant, but there's no doubt still a couple outside. So unless you want this mess still staring at you from the papers at breakfast tomorrow, I suggest you start smiling. I'll take the car in front and field any questions.

And, Millie…' she was walking swiftly beside them to the waiting car '…at least *try* and look as if you've missed him. Levander, hold her hand…the right one…' she directed. 'When you get to the restaurant make sure it's her right hand you're holding.'

He held it, all right—held it so hard it hurt. And despite his insistence that they attend, it was Levander who was flouting the strange rules—marching her to the car just as her father had done at that long-ago party, bundling her into it in a similar fashion, too, not even attempting a smile for the cameras.

'You *knew*…' he gritted as the car sped off towards the restaurant. It was a trip of less than half a kilometre, but there had been no question of walking. 'You deliberately forgot to take it. Well, enjoy the pantomime you've created tonight, Millie. You've clearly worked hard to be here.'

'You're so ready to think the worst of me,' Millie snarled, not caring that they were already pulling into the restaurant, and barely even registering the crowd on the pavement outside. 'Maybe I am thick and stupid, but the fact is I wasn't *on* the pill—and, unlike your usual sophisticates, I don't happen to carry condoms in my purse just in case some bloody six-foot-three Russian decides to come and take my virginity.'

'What?' His voice was hoarse, his eyes darting to Millie's as she tried to look away—anywhere but at him. 'You're telling me—?'

The door was opening on their heated exchange, cameras flashing as their names were called—and she could actually see him hesitate, caught in the desire to shout something rather impolite in Russian, slam the door closed again and carry on what they'd started. But Millie had no intention of continuing this conversation now—or ever, if she could help it.

'That's exactly what I'm telling you,' Millie snapped, before propriety took over and they stepped out of the car. But she delivered one tiny little parting shot for him to chew on over dinner. 'So tell me, Levander, what's *your* excuse?'

CHAPTER SEVEN

'MILLIE!'

'Levander!'

'Over here, Millie!'

As they stepped out of the car and towards the restaurant their names were being called from every angle, and despite the arguments, despite her fury, she clung tightly to his hand—because otherwise she'd surely have turned and run. Though with Katina answering on their behalf, the horror of the press with their blood up was perhaps the lesser of two evils when Levander's family were on the other side of the door, surely furious with this naïve little thing who had got them all into this impossible mess.

The flash of the cameras barely made Levander blink; rather it was her revelation causing shards of glass to explode in front of his eyes. His first instinct was to pull her away from the maddening crowd, to refute her claim, to tell her that the hot, sensual woman he had held that night had known exactly what she was doing, had known exactly how to please a man...

...or how to please *him*.

As they walked the short distance, continuing to be bombarded with questions, he willed himself not to think about her warm body entwined around his, the places they had taken each other that night. Her sweet, tentative, but oh, so tender tongue exploring him, eyes like jewels staring up at him, laced with questions, searching for approval as he'd implored her to go on.

He barely registered the questions that were hurled at them, retracing instead that delicious night—but with guilty feet now, because he *had* thought about a condom.

For the first time Levander admitted that to himself. For that split second as he'd hovered at her entrance, as he'd felt her silky and warm beneath his skilful fingers, it had crossed his mind to reach over as he always did to his bedside table…only he'd *chosen* not to.

Chosen, if not rationally, to allow himself the feel of her. He had given in to want, hollow with a lust that only she could make him feel—the heady release he'd encountered so intense, so vivid, he'd chosen that pleasure.

'Do you or Millie have anything to say about the allegations in the paper this morning regarding a termination?'

It was the one question that stopped him in his tracks—the one question he chose not to ignore.

'Nothing.' Levander disobeyed Katina's orders, not just in his surly response, but by wrapping his left arm around Millie's shoulder and gripping her hand with the other. There wasn't a hope in hell of them getting a shot of the ring—not that Levander seemed to give a damn. His face a picture of contempt as he stared boldly into the crowd. 'There is nothing I want to say to any of you—you all disgust me.'

* * *

It would have been a relief to step inside if his family hadn't been waiting.

And, despite Levander's 'ugly sisters' comment, each was more beautiful than the next. They swooped on her like humming birds—tiny, exquisite women, wrapped in vibrant colours, pecking at her cheek. Though there was nothing fragile in their voices. Despite her complete lack of Russian, Millie knew they were discussing her— thick, rich voices shouted for space as she attempted to centre herself, and she was grateful for the strong hand on her arm as Levander guided her through the maze of the restaurant, led her to the table, where she hoped to draw breath.

'This is my father.'

Millie stared at the most powerful man at the table. Even the best tailor couldn't disguise his emaciated body and gaunt face. Silver hair brushed backwards re- vealed a face that was almost skeletal; shaking hands reached for the glass in front of him.

'My son inherits my love for beautiful women…' He raised a glass in her direction and Millie, unsure of what to do, turned to Levander. But there was no guidance on offer there. Her heart stilled as the anger she had been on the receiving end of paled into insignificance. Like opals on fire, she witnessed the darkness of his eyes turn black as he stared across the table.

'If that is what I am to inherit from you I ask you to strike me off your will,' Levander said coolly, as Millie tried to contain a shocked gasp. 'Your treatment of women is something I hope to avoid.'

'Levander…' Millie couldn't help the scold. The

hatred, the vileness in his voice, was toxic, and to aim it at someone so frail, so publicly, was more than she could comprehend.

'Why do you complain, Levander—I have given you everything—cars, money, yachts…'

'I have worked for them all,' Levander pounced. 'With or without you I would have made it—*vrubatsa?*'

'This much I understand,' Ivan answered. 'Whether or not I live to hear it—one day you will thank me for the opportunities I give you. Without me you are nothing.'

'Without you…' Levander stared across the table, and Millie realised no one was talking; every eye was turned to Levander. 'Is how I have lived my life. Don't ask me to cry for you now. I mourn my mother instead.'

'Levander.' The same throaty voice that had begged him for reason the night they had met was pleading again. 'Papa is sick, but he is here tonight for you. What is wrong with you, Levander? First you shout at Mama this morning…now this.'

What the hell *was* wrong with him? He never referred to the past with his family—with anyone—never let them close enough for that. Yet Annika was right. This was the second time today he had flown at the slightest provocation. Usually he prided himself on the charming yet distant mask he presented to the world, but today he was wearing every emotion on the outside of his skin. Every comment from his family ripped into the wounds he kept carefully hidden; every exchange with Millie delivered an anger he hadn't known since he was a boy.

Downing his drink in one gulp, he had barely hit the glass on the table before the waiter refilled it.

What the hell was he doing?

Tonight was about backing Millie one step further into his corner—to find a way to hold on to her, to ensure she became his bride before she found out about his murky past—and yet here he was, goading his family to reveal the truth they never acknowledged.

His truth.

'Leave it, Annika.' It was Nina who interrupted her daughter. 'This is not the place.'

As a waiter approached and placed a sumptuous seafood platter in front of them, the spitting insults melted into polite chatter, as if nothing had taken place.

'So, when is the wedding?' Nina asked, as Millie took a huge gulp of water.

'We are here, Nina,' Levander answered. 'That is enough.'

'For now.' Nina shrugged. 'You were the one who said to the press she was to be your wife—so now you must decide on a date. We fly to Milan in two weeks—and then on to Paris. Your father needs warm weather now. I think we will see out the European summer there…'

'I really don't need to hear your flight schedule, Nina,' Levander drawled, deliberately missing the point. But Nina was determined to ram it home.

'Sooner is better, Levander—if she is to have a hope of getting into the dress, then you need to get things going.'

The dress.

Nerves catching up, Millie almost giggled, but quickly she swallowed it, knowing not a single one of the Kolovskys would get her humour. Oh, she knew it was Nina's rather limited English that had caused the slip, but Millie had a sudden vision of a wedding dress hanging in a wardrobe somewhere, waiting for any woman with a semblance of a waist to step into it.

'Our wedding is our concern,' Levander said darkly, stopping Nina in her tracks—temporarily at least. But the night just continued in the same bitter vein, and for an already wilting Millie it was beyond confusing.

It was as if she wasn't even there—the charade for the cameras had nothing on this. It was hideous, sitting there while the whole family discussed their relationship as if it were for *them* to decide the outcome. Her cheeks burnt with embarrassment and anger as Nina started talking in Russian—clearly about Millie—rudely gesturing towards her.

The whole table joined in the loud conversation until Levander halted them. 'Millie speaks no Russian—you will speak only in English when she is present.'

'She might not want to hear what we have to say—' one of Nina's sisters attempted.

'All the more reason you should keep quiet,' Levander retorted, and even though his voice was even there was a warning glint in his eye that told all present he wasn't joking—a warning glint in his eye that stayed trained on his stepmother. Millie watched as she flushed, watched as a cruel smile twisted his mouth as Nina finally turned and, with a nervous croak in her voice, addressed her sister.

'We speak English.'

It was awful—the worst meal of her life—and even though she'd only seen them a couple of days ago, Millie was gripped with longing for her own family. The gentle bickering that flared at their dinner table was a million miles from the poisonous atmosphere that shrouded this table. Even more bewildering was the fact that, though Millie spent the meal reeling, Levander seemed completely unfazed, sitting as brooding and as unmoved as he had with his sister on the night they had met, unperturbed by the toxic company…

When the waiter came to take their orders for coffee, she made a last-ditch effort to talk to the reticent Annika.

'You're a designer…?' Millie struggled to make conversation with Levander's stunning half-sister. 'Levander said you mainly do jewellery.'

'I do both jewellery and clothing,' Annika said warily, her eyes darting to her mother.

Levander watched Millie try so hard to fit in with them, and watched as they stonewalled her—just as they had him. He watched them retreat into their diamond-crusted shells when a question might actually demand an answer, watched until it actually hurt to look—till he simply couldn't watch any more.

'Which do you prefer?' Millie went on, and it seemed a perfectly reasonable question—especially from one artist to another—like Nina asking if she preferred to paint with water or oil. But, as Millie was quickly realising, nothing was normal in this family.

'I'm equally good at both.'

'Oh.' Millie floundered, utterly bemused by her response, but accepting it, and steered the conversation to something hopefully more sustainable. 'You were born here? In Australia, I mean?'

'Yes.'

'And do you ever get back…?' Taking a slug of water, and praying they'd hurry with the coffee, Millie glanced over to Levander, who wasn't even attempting to be nice. He appeared thoroughly bored with the night's proceedings. He was glancing at his watch, drumming his fingers on the table as if at any second he might just get up and walk out. Hopefully he'd remember to take her with him, Millie thought darkly, as she attempted to get this wary woman to at least make small talk.

'To Russia?' Millie's wide smile was so strained, so forced, she could almost feel her lips splitting under the strain. 'To…' She gave a tiny frown as she tried to recall the name Levander had cited. 'To Detsky Dom?'

If she'd stood up and danced naked on the table, if she'd passed wind and laughed, the response couldn't have been worse. Annika knocked over her wine glass as she let out a shocked gasp, Nina just gaped at her for her boldness, and Ivan spluttered into a noisy fit of coughing. But most curious of all, as she turned anguished eyes to Levander for support, as she tried and failed to understand what on earth she had said that was so awful, she was stunned to see him put back his head and laugh.

'I'm sorry,' Millie floundered helplessly. 'What did I say?'

'Don't be sorry.' Still Levander laughed, but his eyes when he stood were as black as coal. 'You see—Annika is too good for Detsky Dom—is that not right, Nina? Come…' As the waiter placed a shot of espresso in front of him, Levander didn't even give it a glance. 'We go now.'

'It is too soon—' Nina started, but Levander was adamant.

'Why?' Levander challenged. 'You have your pictures for the paper.'

And so it started again—scarlet lips air-kissing her cheeks, perfume wafting in her nostrils as the table noisily farewelled them. And if she'd been confused before, Mille was perturbed now, her head whirring with questions as they stepped out of the restaurant and into a waiting car—sped the few hundred metres to the hotel and in a matter of moments were back in Levander's sumptuous suite.

'What did I say wrong?' She was shaken to the core, but her voice was somehow strong. 'I don't understand.'

'You never will with my family.'

'They were so rude…' If the rules stated that no matter how much your partner did, one should never criticise his family, then it was way too late. 'And yet when we stood up to go…'

'Others were watching,' Levander elucidated, and for Millie it was just too much. She shook her head in astonishment as Levander continued darkly, 'What you just witnessed was a first-class production Kolovsky-style. All they care about is reputation—and how we appear to others. The truth matters nothing to any of them.'

'You were rude, too…' Millie said accusingly. 'From the second we got in there you were poisonous. Why don't you like him? Because he left your mother?'

'Leave it, Millie.'

'And Nina,' Millie insisted, recalling the hate in his

eyes, the cruel smile on his lips. 'You don't just dislike her, do you? You actually *hate* her.'

How, Levander asked himself, did she do it? How did she know to ask the one thing he couldn't answer? He could deal with a boardroom full of questions, deal with his family with his eyes closed, fob them off with half-answers, yet with her he wanted more than anything to confide in her, to give her the answers she sought. He had to crunch his hands into fists, so tempted was he to take hers, to finally share his hell.

But how could he?

'It is complicated.' Levander closed his eyes as he tried to come up with a suitable answer, trying to buy himself just a little more time till she was his to tell. 'It is family business—my father's story as much as mine.'

'Well, given I'm carrying his grandchild, when *am* I allowed to know?' She watched his face quilt with tension. She didn't want another row, but she wanted to know what the hell was going on. 'He's not just sick, is he…?'

'No, he's not just sick; he's dying—happy now?'

'Happy?' She shook her head in disbelief at his coldness, reeling at the impossibility of him—the memory of the tenderness that she had surely once seen in him was dimming further with every bitter twist of his tongue. 'Your father's dying and you talk to him like that…'

'I said leave it, Millie.'

'I wanted to leave it.' Millie was shouting now. 'I *wanted* to leave it, but you were the one who sent me into that minefield—I want to know—'

'*Men'she znayesh'-krepche spish'.*' He shouted his answer in Russian, which really was no answer at all, but his voice was so hoarse, so angry, so full of pain it scared her—only not for herself, for him. 'You need to go to bed.'

'You're really good at telling me what I need to do—especially when I ask a question that you don't want to answer.'

She scared him—not the little five-foot-three ball of anger who stood angry and defiant before him now, but the woman she was, the questions she asked. And more than that it was the feelings she triggered—dangerous feelings that confused him, made him think he must somehow be losing his mind...

'Go to bed...' His voice was a croak, but his actions were insistent and he guided her to the bedroom.

It should have been familiar, but in the few hours they'd been away the bed had been re-made and turned down—strangers had crept in and changed the landscape again. That Levander wanted her gone rather than try to talk things through, explain his family to her, was for Millie the worst. With a sob of frustration she headed to the bathroom, ripping the beastly clips out of her hair, pulling off the Kolovsky silk dress and leaving it in a crumpled heap on the floor.

Not even bothering to take off her make-up, too angry to even tie up her robe, she wrapped a towel around her and stormed back into the bedroom as he was heading out of the door. 'You know...jealousy really doesn't suit you, Levander.'

'You don't know what you're talking about.'

'Oh, but I think I do—you're jealous of them, aren't you?' She watched his face whiten, watched a muscle leaping in his cheek as she taunted him with vicious words—furious, hurt-fuelled words for the way he had treated her. She was missing the man she had met oh, so briefly, and hating what he had become. 'You're jealous that while you had to struggle on the other side of the world the rest of your family was living in luxury.'

'You think I am *jealous?*' He spat out a mirthless laugh. 'You think *that* is what makes me like this? Well, then—you don't know me at all.'

'I'm trying to,' Millie shouted. 'But at every turn you silence me with your mouth. Kissing me, sending me to bed, answering me in Russian... What does it *mean?*' she jeered. 'Come on—what you said before; what does it mean?'

'I can't even remember what I said...'

'Men'she znayesh'—krepche spish.' She watched his hand tighten around the door handle as she said it—his back stiffened, the muscles across his shoulders so taut she could have bounced a ball off them. His expression was unreadable when finally he turned around. He must have thought she'd have forgotten, but the words, even if they hadn't been understood, had been so hollow, so full of hurt, they'd stay with her for ever.

'Okay, then—it is a Russian saying—a proverb...' He couldn't even look at her as he spoke, and perhaps she'd misread him—because he looked more jaded than bitter, more resigned now than angry. And somehow, even though she was standing there, even though they had been with his family tonight, never had she seen someone look more alone. 'It means—*the less you know, the more soundly you sleep.*'

'But what if I *want* to know?' Before she had even finished speaking he had left, closing the door behind him. And even though there was no turn of a key Millie knew, *knew* Levander was locking her out.

Over and over she replayed the night—reviewed his short but brutal history. Simultaneously she recalled the tiny snippets she'd gleaned, like ominous thick drops of rain pelting on a windscreen, warning her of an impending storm: Annika's horrified reaction when she'd spoken of his home town, his sudden arrival in Australia, his odd relationship with his father and his family, and his clear bemusement when she'd questioned his choice of home.

The truth she had so desperately sought was less than appealing now as realisation hit that in her search for answers she'd missed out on a question—had taken for granted the misinformation she'd been fed. She had never actually asked Levander *when* his mother had died.

Dressed in nothing more than a silk wrap, Millie pushed open the bedroom door and saw him standing, staring unseeing out of the window, more beautiful than any model in art class, so still, so tense, so loaded with pain it made her want to weep.

He didn't even turn his head—didn't move a muscle as she approached.

'How old were you?' She didn't need to elaborate, knew when he closed his eyes that he understood the question. But she waited an age before finally he gave his hollow answer.

'Three.'

'So, when she died, did her family…?' She couldn't go on for a moment. She wanted so much for him to interrupt her, to tell her that whatever she was thinking surely she was wrong. 'Did they raise you?'

'They would have had to take food out of their own child's mouth to do that... You do not understand poor...' He wasn't being derisive or scathing, Millie realised. Quite simply he was stating a fact. Her lips trembled in horror. She was trying not to cry, and somehow to absorb the information he was giving her— because even if she didn't know Russian...no guessing was needed now.

'Detsky Dom isn't a town, is it...?' Her hand reached for him, fingers gentle on his taut shoulders. 'When she died you were put in a children's home.'

'No.'

For the first time since she'd come into the room he looked at her, or rather towards her. His eyes were fixed on her, perhaps, but somehow not focusing. His voice was detached and formal, and listening to him, watching his tense mouth form the most vile of words, was like being plunged into boiling water—like blistering pain on every cell of her skin as she tried and failed to fathom all he must have been through.

'Before she died, when she was too sick to look after me, I was put in *dom rebyonka*—the baby house. Later, when I was four, I went to *detsky dom*.'

There was nothing she could say.

A million questions for later, maybe, but there was nothing she could say now...

'And, no—before you suggest it again—I am *not* jealous. I accept the past, and the impossible choices that were made. I accept what they cannot.'

'I don't understand.'

'How could you?' His voice was hollow. 'Now your curiosity is satisfied—perhaps it is better you go…'

'Go?' Her hand was on his arm and she could feel him now—could *feel* him. For a second or two she hadn't been able to, hadn't been able to feel anything at all. Shock was a kind of anaesthetic at times, blocking the pain that consumed her, numbing everything in its wake. Only feelings were creeping in now. The two of them were still there, still standing after his revelation. That he would push her away after she'd forced her way in was almost more than she could bear. 'Why do you want me to go…?'

Because you will.

He didn't say it, just stared—stared at eyes swollen from the tears he'd provoked at the once happy face, now devoid of her ever-ready smile—and hated himself for tainting her, for soiling what had once been perfect.

'It is better if you go to bed.'

It really wasn't her place to argue, Millie realised, pulling her hand back. She respected his decision and turned to go, because it wasn't her place to tell him how he should feel, to say that whatever he privately thought of her surely at this moment he shouldn't be alone.

'I'm sorry.' Those two words had surely never sounded so paltry, but they came from the bottom of her heart. 'I'm sorry for all you must have been through.'

She turned to go, then changed her mind—and leant forward to kiss him. It was with the least provocative of intentions—a kiss goodnight she would give to any mortal in agony, any friend who had bared a piece of their soul.

Only he wasn't a friend.

Leaning over him and dusting his lips with comfort had been the intention. But when she felt his lips beneath hers, that quick kiss goodnight lingered just a fraction too long. So easy to kiss, so easy to close her eyes as she did and chase away the atrocities... A sweeter feeling was rushing in, replacing the horror, but after a moment of indulgence she felt his hands on her shoulders, felt him pushing her back.

'This time...' His voice wasn't quite so detached now, and his breath was hard and ragged between each reluctant word. 'When I suggest you go to bed I trust you understand I am not angry...'

'I do.'

She did.

Absolutely she understood what he was saying.

And absolutely she understood the balmy sedative she was offering.

'If you want me to stay then I will.' Her voice was different, unfamiliar even to Millie. Wanton words from very deliberate lips as she offered him this—and it wasn't just for Levander, but for her.

She didn't want to visit his nightmare, yet—didn't want to lie alone in her bed and weep for his past. She wanted him *now*—wanted the escape she was offering too. She could feel the rise and fall of his chest against hers. Her hands were filled with a shameful longing to move down, to feel what she knew was surely there—surely, because he was struggling to look at her, struggling to push her away as their bodies screamed otherwise.

It would be impossible to walk with legs that felt like jelly, but somehow she'd manage it. The bedroom door was a blur in the distance, the room so thick with tension she'd need a scythe to get there—but if he told her to go again then she would.

He didn't.

Didn't say anything at all. Instead his mouth crushed hers in response, in a fierce, desperate kiss that slammed the breath out of her, that exactly matched her need. A kiss that hurt with its intensity—a delicious hurt, though. His skin rough on hers, his tongue probing, his arms dragging her tightly to him, but not close enough for Millie. Her silk wrap slipping off her shoulders, she grabbed at his shirt, ripping away the material so that naked she could press against him—feel his hard arousal beneath his trousers as his hands cupped her bottom, the metal of his zipper digging into her.

'All-day-since-I-saw-you...' Between kisses he spoke, with his mouth full sometimes...full of her mouth, her shoulder, her breast. His tongue explored the changes since last he'd visited, each stroke a fever on her ripe, needy flesh, each husky word from his lips refuting his earlier contempt, giddying her, yet propelling her towards a rapidly approaching destination. 'All-day-I-am-hard-for-you.'

So hard.

Desperate fingers pulled at his zipper, needy hands freeing his heated length. She wanted to linger just a second, but Levander wasn't having any of it. Strong

hands around her waist lifted her those necessary decadent inches and her legs coiled around his back. She
bit into his shoulder as he plunged inside her, gasped as
he filled her, not knowing what to do. But again he
showed her, his hands guiding her bottom into a delicious rhythm, thrusting till she found her own. And it
was so much more than sex for the sake of it—because
if ever comfort was needed it was tonight—and if all
they had was this, then surely they must build on it.

'I cannot last…'

His apology was a second overdue. Millie was the first
to arrive—and in fabulous style, with a flash of heat searing up her spine so intense and so unexpected it startled
her. Her new-found boldness utterly gone, she locked
shocked eyes with his, feeling a flash of fear as she faced
the unknown. But it was Levander holding her, telling her
with his eyes that it was all okay, just different. With a
squeal of delighted terror she let herself go with it…gave
the little piece of her heart that was left to him.

CHAPTER EIGHT

IF MILLIE had thought that his revelations, the fabulous sex, or even the fact that Levander was now firmly instated in the bedroom would mean they were closer, she was wrong on each count.

It was as if he'd never touched her—and certainly as if he'd never told her anything. The topic of his past was once again completely out of bounds. Brooding, impossible and utterly unreachable, he rumbled like a prolonged peal of thunder through his inhuman schedule. Up at the crack of dawn to go running, then out to face his brutal day. And rather than talking, or spending their time getting closer, instead she was paraded to endless business dinners followed by even more endless parties. Yes, he slept beside her—and sometimes in sleep he even reached out and held her—but he never actually laid a finger on her, and night after night she lay miserable in her own desire, staring at the man who said he wanted to marry her, yet didn't seem to like her very much at all.

'I rather like this one.'

At the end of the week, as Katina handed them both

individual copies of the same newspaper, Millie winced again as she re-read the headline that had hit the stands on her second day in town: *From London with Love.*

'In fact, all the newspaper reports have been favourable. I've also managed a sneak peek at some of the magazines out next week and, though I'm loath to say it, Levander, your rather surly interaction with the press seems to have them eating out of your hands... Paragraph two,' she clipped, like a schoolteacher, as she handed them yet another article. '"*Kolovsky appeared defensive of his young fiancée, shielding her from the press and clearly eager to get inside to share the moment with his family.*" The two of you have done very well, and as a surprising bonus it's taken the attention away from your father's illness. I'd say they're all pretty much scrambling to break the happy news of your wedding date—so when can I tell them it is?'

'When I find out—' Levander gave a tight smile '—you'll be the first to hear.'

'Well?' Katina's very trim rear had hardly wiggled out of the room when Levander tossed the question at her.

'Gosh, you can be so romantic at times, Levander. I told you I wasn't going to be pushed into anything.' She ran a worried hand over her forehead. 'Look, I've got this "meet the artist" thing with Anton, and after that...' Biting her bottom lip, she forced herself to look at him. 'After that, I think I ought to go home for a bit—you know, talk to my family...' He didn't say anything. She'd braced herself for the rip of his words, or the crack of his temper, but he just sat there, staring at her coolly, making her squirm with discomfort. If anything, it was far worse. 'I need to go home and decide what I should do.'

'You *know* what you should do.'

She gave a tiny helpless laugh. 'Sign my life away to a loveless marriage…'

'It does not mean it would not be a good marriage.'

'We don't talk.'

'We're talking now,' came his flip response.

'You don't tell me how you feel…'

'Why would I?' He looked at her as if it were so bloody obvious he couldn't believe she had a problem with it. 'Why-would-I-tell-you?'

'So we can get closer…' Millie shivered. 'So we can…' She had to be brave, had to ask him, *had* to know. 'Do you think…I don't know…in time…?' She was trying not to cry, trying not to sound needy, but the memory of his cast-off lover came to mind as she heard shades of the Latina's pleading creeping into her voice. But, hell, there was a baby to think of—so she squared herself to ask the most difficult question of all. Difficult, Millie realised, because if you actually had to ask, you probably weren't going to like the answer. 'Do you think you could ever love me?'

'My God…' he muttered under his breath, as if she were some stupid little girl who bored him with senseless questions, each incredulous shake of his head humiliating her right to her core. 'Always this question comes—" Levander, do you love me?" "Levander, if I change this maybe then you will love me?" "Levander… why can't you just *say* you love me…?" I am not going to lie to you and tell you I think I will be in love with you. I cannot say that.'

'I get the message.' She halted him with a shaking hand, her tense face splitting into a rueful smile, tears stinging at the back of her nose, wishing he would stop. But Levander hadn't even started.

'You know, I don't think you do—so I make this clear. You are not a prisoner—your passport is in the safe and you know the combination. Walk out through that door—go back to England—the choice is yours.'

'I just need to think,' Millie said helplessly. 'I'm not saying no to marriage…'

She was going. It was all he could hear—all that consumed him. All week he'd been waiting, knowing that now she knew the truth of what he was she would leave him. She was going and taking his baby, and as sure as night followed day Levander knew she wouldn't be coming back. The second she got home, back to her family, they'd claim her, talk to her, tell her just how much she didn't need him.

She was going—and he'd move heaven and earth to stop her walking through that door. He didn't deserve her, but he couldn't let her go.

'You try to keep me from this baby—I warn you how it will be.' Once again his deepening accent signalled his inner emotional turmoil. His eyes were as black as the darkest night as he fought with the gloves off. 'It is *your* shame that was smeared over the newspapers—*your* talk of ending the pregnancy that is documented. You are the one walking out on a chance of giving our child a stable home—you deny my child a chance to properly get to know its father. See how far you get.'

'I don't understand…'

'Then I will explain better,' Levander sneered. 'You are some two-bit artist who when we met hadn't sold so much as a painting. There is one advantage to being a Kolovsky—money—and if I have to work in the family business for ever I will do it—if I have to spend every last cent ensuring my child is brought up beside his father I will.'

'Levander…' Fear was licking at the edges—real fear. His demands were so unreasonable it was almost impossible to fathom that he was serious. But he was. If she went back to England then she'd be plunged into hell: her private life spewed across the papers, endless lawyers and bills and fighting… But how, after issuing such threats, could he possibly expect her to stay?

'We'll go away.'

His voice was hoarse. As quickly as that he had changed. He had been a ball of lightning, rolling towards her, hissing anger and singeing all in its wake, but suddenly his anger had dispersed, replaced with an urgency that scared her on a different level—it scared her for *him*. For just a split second she glimpsed the little boy he must have been—the scared child whose life had been ripped away from him by the untimely death of his mother. Then the shutters came down, but he continued softly, urgently.

'Right now. We'll go somewhere we can talk. I will arrange it now—we will go this afternoon. I will try…'

His eyes were imploring her to listen, to just please hear him out, two black holes of dark emotion as he offered her the impossible. 'I will try to let you know me.'

CHAPTER NINE

'NEARLY there now.'

They'd barely spoken the whole journey, but Millie didn't mind. As they'd headed for the fabulous tropical north, leaving the cool southern winter behind, the silence had at first been strained, then mutual. Both were lost in their thoughts, both trying to comprehend the magnitude of whatever lay ahead. Slowly, as the plane had gobbled up the miles, the tension had seeped out of them, and by the time they arrived at Great Barrier Reef Airport, where they boarded a seaplane to take them for the final leg of their journey, they were actually managing to string together a few words.

Millie's face was pressed to the window. She was taking in the azure of the water, so clear she could see the fish, and occasionally lush green islands rushing beneath them like some fabulous holiday brochure.

'Are you okay?'

'Fine,' Millie breathed. 'But cross with myself.'

'Cross?'

'I should have made the effort to get up here the

first time. I can't believe I might have missed out on seeing this.'

'You haven't seen anything yet.'

He wasn't exaggerating.

A small speedboat greeted them, taking them on their last journey, sweeping them up to the beach—and it was like stepping into paradise as Levander helped her out. Cool water lapped around her ankles, and a gentle breeze skimmed over the Pacific Ocean, heralding the arrival of dusk. The endless white sand was so soft and powdery it was as inviting as a bed, and beyond low wooden huts blended so carefully with the forest of trees that at first glance they were missed entirely.

'This whole island belongs to your family?'

'It does. This was one of my father's wiser decisions—he bought it for a song when mortgage rates soared and everyone was going under. At the time he couldn't afford it, of course, but now...'

'It's amazing,' Millie breathed.

'I come here a lot.' She heard the full stop, and watched as he faltered, as he visibly attempted to do what he had promised to do—let her in to his thoughts. 'Mainly I come alone—here I seem to relax.'

'I can see why.' Millie smiled. 'It's just stunning.'

'It is,' Levander said simply, taking her elbow and leading her along the beach to a vast hut, along its decking and through a vast marabou door.

Though it was simply furnished it too was stunning—massive white sofas, beneath a whirring ceiling fan, the focal point of the lounge. All the shutters on the windows were open and the setting sun streamed hues of orange against the white walls. Endless white sofas were littered with cushions, family photos adorned surfaces and walls—it was way more intimate than the lavish hotel Levander called home.

Millie took her time looking at the photos, smiling at a younger Levander, serious and scowling at a family wedding—but even as she smiled it tore at her heart. His undocumented childhood had never been more evident as she stared at dark-haired, dark-eyed twins racing around on tricycles, and Annika too, blonde and gorgeous, beaming out of her pram.

'Is that you?' Millie jumped at the prospect, picking up a black and white baby photo and staring at the solemn eyes and the thatch of dark hair.

'That is my father.' Levander glanced over. 'I am not so old that I wore a dress as a baby.'

'He looks like you.' Millie laughed. 'Or rather, you look like *him*. I wonder…' A shiver of the most unexpected excitement rippled through her. The fleeting maternal impulses that had seen her through to date were beating more strongly now, coursing through her and settling to a rhythm, thrumming into a beat, as she surveyed this magnificent gene pool—as the baby deep inside her was fashioned into more than a possibility. An almost tangible image was teasing her mind's eye as she merged their features.

'I wonder too.' Levander finished her sentence for her. 'Since I found out I have wondered if he will be blond…' She opened her mouth to correct him, but Levander spoke over her. 'Or if she will be dark.'

'What would you like?' Millie asked. 'I mean, I know

it doesn't matter, but if you could choose, what would you like our baby to be…?'

He really seemed to think about it—frowning at her question, then shaking his head.

'I'll think about it and let you know.'

Which was rather a strange answer, but she didn't dwell on it. Her mouth had dropped open as for the first time she saw her picture—the one she herself had painted.

'You shouldn't have done that…' Even if he'd meant well, even if he'd done it for all the right reasons, still it was wrong. Her hard-fought-for success seemed not so worthy now. 'We both agreed that that would be cheating.'

'There was no cheating. I followed up with the lady who bought it. She was happy with my price.'

'Oh.'

He heard her little thud of disappointment and smiled. 'She is an art dealer, Millie—she bought it to sell it on. You are going to have to get used to that. People will not always buy your work for sentimental reasons.'

'So why did you?' Her cheeks flushed as she asked, a tiny glow flickering inside as she awaited his answer. But it was soon doused when Levander shrugged and then stared at the picture.

'It interests me, I suppose…' He peered a bit more closely. 'Really I have never invested in art. But perhaps I will think about it now…'

'So it's just us here?' Millie checked, changing the subject, trying to hide her disappointment, kicking herself for expecting anything more and staring beyond to the vast view outside. 'Well, apart from the staff.'

She could see them on the beach—setting up a table,

lighting a fire—but Levander had promised seclusion and he really meant it.

'They will leave soon—they come twice a day while there are guests.

'Do they live here on the island?'

'No—there…' He headed to a window and pointed at some glittering lights, seemingly miles away. "That is a luxury hotel, some ten kilometres away. The staff are from there.'

'So, no Room Service at night?' Millie said, blowing her fringe skywards as she let out a breath and reeled at the opulence of the Kolovskys' existence, trying and failing to see how she could ever even begin to belong.

'If you want something, then I'm sure it can be arranged.' There was a distinctive edge to his voice. 'I'll go and tell them we're ready to eat. Would you like to shower before dinner?'

Even in the middle of nowhere—even in the most romantic setting on God's earth—it would seem there were still formalities to be observed. Still there was protocol to follow if you were dining with a Kolovsky.

'Of course.' Mille gave a tight smile. 'I shan't be long.'

She'd spent that morning in a spending frenzy. Utterly unable to stomach another Kolovsky freebie, she'd taken a thoroughly excited Anton on a shopping spree—though he'd been initially less than delighted to learn she would have to postpone her 'meet the artist' night—and had spent half her earnings to date on what she hoped was a suitably fantastic holiday wardrobe. It seemed to have helped him get over his disappointment.

Now making her way into the bedroom, ready to pull out the few inches of gold fabric Anton had selected from her suitcase, Millie blinked at the impeccable room. After a moment she realised there would be no unpacking. It had all been taken care of—her new clothes were hanging neatly in the wardrobe, her new shoes were neatly arranged on the floor, her perfume, make-up, even her hair straighteners were all neatly arranged in the fabulous bathroom.

The Kolovskys' attempt at low key made her swoon in wonder. Everything was cool white, from the floor-to-ceiling marble to the fluffy white robe and towels, and one wall entirely taken up with the biggest mirror Millie had ever seen—it was like stepping into a movie set. She wanted to fill the bath with bubbles and sink into it. But worried her hair would frizz, she pulled on a cap and settled for a quick shower instead. After that she pulled on her very new, very expensive, not particularly comfortable underwear—but the effect was surely worth it, Millie thought. She picked up her dress and pulled the raw silk over her head, the luxurious material hugging the curves of her body as she stepped back to check herself in the mirror.

Pregnancy was certainly starting to wreak its changes on her body. Her breasts, which had always bordered on generous, were like two ripe peaches now—and just as bruisable. The tender nipples were like two thistles sticking out under her dress, and nothing was going to slim down the curve of her buttocks to the supermodel proportions he was no doubt used to.

And yet…

…she felt beautiful.

The strange, slightly angular jut of her stomach as she stood side on fascinated her.

Pressing her hand against the dress, Millie closed her eyes. Instead of a soft, doughy mound of tummy, she was greeted instead with a hard wedge of flesh.

'Does it move?'

He made her jump, but Millie gave a resigned sigh—since when would a closed bathroom door stop a man like Levander?

'The baby, I mean,' Levander elaborated when Millie failed to answer, a touch embarrassed that he had caught her staring at herself.

'It was jumping around like anything on the scan.' Millie smiled at the memory. 'But I don't think I can feel it yet. The doctor said not for a few more weeks.'

'You don't *think* you can feel it?'

'Sometimes…' Millie gave a rueful smile at her own imagination. 'Sometimes I think I feel a little flutter, but the doctor said it was probably just—' She chose not to go on. She didn't really want to discuss her digestive system with him. But it was nice that he was so interested—nice that he wasn't angry, or mocking, or any of the other hateful things he could so often be. 'Do you want to feel?' Beneath her foundation she was blushing to her roots, but comfortable with her decision all the same. Sex was utterly off her agenda till this entire mess was sorted, but *this* wasn't about *that*. 'I mean, there's nothing to actually feel, but…'

'I would love to.'

His hand through her dress was thankfully more

intimate than sexy. Even if her bump wasn't exactly spectacular, he ran a fascinated hand over her and it was his moment to keep. His hand moved up and cupped the soft jut of her stomach so tentatively that Millie gave a soft laugh.

'You won't feel anything like that; here—' She pressed his hand in harder, pushing his index finger in between her pubic bone and her tummy button, just enough so that he could feel the firm ridge of her uterus, and she stared down at their entwined hands. The glitter of the diamond on her finger caught her eye. It was a diamond given for the wrong reasons, but somehow it felt right that it was there. And she knew from the way he held her, from the intent concentration and wonder on his face, that come what may her baby would always have a father, that whatever transpired between them Levander would be in this child's life for ever.

'I would like our baby to be happy.' Levander smiled at her confusion at his unexpected statement. 'I was thinking about what you asked, and I guess if our baby is happy we will have done a good job.'

She'd meant would he want a boy or a girl—had thought surely he had understood that—yet the answer he gave was exactly the right one. Strange that it brought tears to her eyes…

'Everything is local produce.'

A waiter was ladling barramundi onto her plate. The tangy citrus of lime reached her nostrils, and tiny, heavily buttered baby potatoes tossed through caramelised shallots soaked up the fragrant juices. She felt the strategically lit fire warming her bare shoulders as the smoke drifted down-wind.

'It looks fabulous.'

It tasted it too, and under any other circumstances Millie would have closed her eyes and relished the cocktail of taste on her tongue. Under any other circumstances perhaps she would then have opened them and gazed in awe at her dining partner…

…just not this one.

As the waiter melted into the shadows Millie chanced a peek from under her curled and blackened eyelashes and rued the promise of make-up.

Truly impeccable features could only ever be enhanced by nature—and the low half-moon hanging like a strategic lantern in the navy sky did the job perfectly, shadowing his jawline, the jut of his exquisite cheekbones slicing through his face, over the dark, suspicious eyes that watched her.

'Do they have to be here?'

"Who?' Levander frowned.

'The staff,' Millie attempted, leaning forward, speaking in a low whisper, afraid that the waiter might hear what she was saying. 'I just don't feel we can really talk…'

'They are not listening to us.'

'Rubbish,' Millie retorted. 'I've been a waitress, remember—your waitress—and look where we ended up.'

'I can dismiss them for tonight, if it makes you more comfortable. If you are not happy with the service, I will tell them to be more discreet, to—'

'The service is fabulous…fabulous,' Millie said, her

urgent whisper drifting across the table. 'But we might as well be sitting in a restaurant in Melbourne, or London, or anywhere on the globe…'

'I don't get you, Millie—I tell you I am taking you away, somewhere we will not be disturbed, you disappear for three hours, come back with your hair done and a whole new wardrobe. You are no sooner here than you moan there will be no room service…'

'I was being—' Millie attempted, but Levander spoke over her.

'You put on a gold dress for dinner, and use a trowel for your make-up, and now you complain that you want low-key.'

God, he could be so brutal at times!

'I don't know how I'm supposed to be with you, Levander,' she returned, salty, glitter-filled tears spilling down her cheeks. 'I know *myself* is the obvious answer, but since you came along I don't know who I am any more. I just hoped it would be the two of us.'

He didn't say anything. Just stood up from the table and headed over to the waiter, speaking in low tones Millie couldn't hear before rejoining her.

'They are leaving. There are enough provisions in the cupboards and freezers; I do not have staff when I am here by myself. I just wasn't sure what you would want.'

'Touché.' Millie sniffed, then managed a watery smile. 'You could have at least waited till they'd cleared up after dinner. I'm joking,' she added, in case he thought she was being precious.

'We met when you were clearing tables—and if you

had any idea of the effect you have on me, you'd know how delighted I am to farewell the staff.'

It was dark enough that he couldn't see her blush, but it was a dangerous hint of a flirt and it worried her. Till they'd sorted out this mess, he'd jolly well better forget about any of *that*.

As the staff packed up and headed to the speedboat, as its engine faded into the distance, Millie felt a shiver—not of excitement, but of nervousness. Nowhere on earth could they be more isolated—now it really was just the two of them, with no distractions or duties to cloud the issue, no background chatter or waiters hovering.

Stuck on a desert island with the man she loved—the same man who'd told her outright that he'd never love *her.*

CHAPTER TEN

EVEN without the intrusion of staff—even though they were quite literally, quite unbelievably, on a desert island and the purpose of their trip here was to talk—it couldn't just happen on demand.

Despite all her best efforts to relax, on the first morning Millie was impossibly awkward—up early, she slathered herself in sunblock, then dressed in a bikini, shorts, T-shirt and sandals. She banged into Levander at every turn in the vast kitchen as she fixed breakfast, trying to avert her eyes as he wandered around in a very low-slung towel, even more impossibly gorgeous than usual, yawning and stretching and drinking milk straight from the carton as she rigidly chopped fruit.

'Do you want fruit salad?'

'No.' He leant over and took a slab of watermelon, his lazy eyes taking in her clothes, before smiling at her pursed lips. 'Can you get a newspaper from the shop when you go?'

'What shop?' Millie asked, then instantly regretted it. She realised he was teasing her for being so over-dressed and gritted her teeth, slicing faster.

'I'm going for a swim—coming?'

'No.' He was walking out through the door…the door that led to the beach, not the bedroom…and yet she was just so appalled at the prospect that she couldn't stand it, couldn't stand it a second longer. She was terrified he'd expect them to run around naked, like in some awful nudist colony…

'Levander—'

'Whoops—'

The two words were said at the time.

Levander turned slow and lazy towards her, giving her a very nice smile. 'I nearly forgot to get my bathers.'

'Pig,' Millie mouthed at the gorgeous sight of his departing back, reeling at the change in him. Without his family, without the press, he was like the man she had fallen head over heels for on their very first night—*better* even than the man she had met on their very first night. But she was still furious with him for his hateful manner in Melbourne. Furious with him for the game he was playing. Furious with him for teasing. Furious with herself for still wanting him so.

Sitting scowling and burning on the beach, watching Levander churning the surf with impossibly strong strokes, wasn't going to help matters. When he was far enough out she took off her T-shirt and sandals, telling herself it was silly to be so shy. But she couldn't even contemplate taking the top of her bikini off and going for an even tan. After all they'd done he'd already seen everything, but she'd never felt fatter or paler or more exposed, sitting on a vast beach in a tiny red bikini and watching him rise like some sexy Greek god from the water. And he was definitely sexy when wet, Millie thought, watching from behind her sunglasses as he walked over and proceeded to shake himself like shaggy dog, dripping water all over her.

'The water is nice.'

'Good.'

'You should go in.'

'I might mess up my make up,' she spat back—even though she wasn't wearing any.

'I'm sorry for what I said…' He smiled at her petulance. 'You actually looked very beautiful last night.'

'Thanks for telling me *now!*'

'I have learnt to fight dirty…' His admission halted her a fraction. 'I had to in order to survive—not just with my family, but before. I will try not to do it to you again.' He lowered himself down beside her. He didn't bother with a towel or anything, just laid his wet body on the sand and stared, squinting, up at the sun. 'You don't fight dirty—do you?'

She stared down at him as he asked, and it was easier somehow to look at him, to answer him, with her sunglasses on. 'I've never had to.'

'I've spent all this time thinking you are like them— like the others—but I realise now that you're nothing like them at all…'

'Why does this have to be a fight, Levander?' She frowned in bemusement, working hard to understand him. 'Why—when surely we both want the same thing for our child.'

'A family?' he asked, and behind her glasses she

screwed her eyes closed unable to answer his impassioned plea. 'That is what I want.'

It was Levander who broke the impossible silence. 'How did *your* family take the news?'

'They were shocked.' Millie gulped. 'Stunned, really. It was just the last thing they expected. I've always been so…'

'Cautious?' Levander offered, thinking of his own family's perpetual warnings.

'Not cautious.' Millie frowned. 'More—driven, I guess. Since high school, art's been my passion. My trip to Australia took months to arrange. The only dream I've ever really had is painting. Unlike most parents, when they waved me off the possibility of their daughter coming home pregnant was the furthest thing from their minds.'

'When did you tell them?'

'About a month ago.' Millie let out a long, shaky breath, then opened her mouth to carry on, and found that she couldn't just yet. But Levander didn't push. Instead, in his most surprising move since he'd grabbed her into that first fierce embrace at the airport, he wrapped his hand around hers, held it gently for a moment or two. It helped—really helped. Drawing from his quiet support, she was ready to continue.

'When I got back from Australia, after a couple of weeks I plucked up the courage and went to a clinic—you know, to get checked…'

'There was no need,' Levander said. 'It was a first for me too, without…'

She couldn't really tell with her glasses on, but Millie could have sworn he was blushing a touch—and she was too, just recalling the mortification she'd felt, sitting waiting for her unlucky number to be called.

'Well, I didn't know that at the time,' Millie said with a tight smile. 'But, yes, the only test I failed was the pregnancy one. I didn't know how to tell them at first, and even when I did I didn't tell them it was a...' She swallowed hard before saying it. 'A one-night stand. I sort of let them think—well, that we cared.'

'We do.' It was perhaps the single nicest thing he'd said to her. 'What else did you tell them?'

'I said that...' Blushing, cringing, she could hardly bring herself to say it.

'You'd better tell me.' He smiled over at her embarrassment. 'If I am going to meet them, perhaps I should know.'

'I said that your family owned a shop near Anton's gallery.'

'A shop?'

'A little shop.' Millie cringed again.

'So they think I am the local greengrocer's son?' He was joking, but seeing her anguished expression he realised *she* wasn't. 'You're not serious?'

'Well, not a greengrocer's. I said that they ran a clothes shop. Obviously they know the truth now.'

'But why would you not tell them in the first place? Surely it could only have made things easier...'

'Or scarier for them.'

He stilled beside her.

'This is their grandchild, Levander. Knowing who you are, how powerful you could be...well, I guess they'll be scared for the same reasons I am.'

'I don't want to fight you, Millie.'

'Then don't.' Regretting the warning note in her voice, she sought diversion. She didn't want to push things to another ugly head—here was their chance to find each other. 'Let's paddle.'

'Paddle?' Levander frowned. 'The boats are…'

'Paddle.' Millie laughed. 'With our feet.'

He had no idea what she was talking about, Millie realised, taking him by the hand towards the lapping foreshore—had no idea what it was to stand in the surf and just enjoy the heavy pull of salt water as it gushed around your ankles.

A playboy who didn't now how to play.

But he learnt quickly.

She'd braved Brighton in an English summer, so it was really nothing to throw off her inhibitions, take his hand and run screaming into the warm Pacific Ocean. Just one bemused frown from Levander, as she skidded a fistful of water in his direction, then he quickly caught on and skidded one back. They played in the water like carefree children, Levander spluttering with laughter as she dived underneath and caught his ankles. She held her breath as he had his revenge, ducking her under, and then his strong thighs caught around her and pulled her up to the surface. She gulped in air—until his mouth caught hers, kissing her so hard, so fiercely her head swam. Not from lack of oxygen but from the sheer intensity of his kiss.

'This we do well…'

'We do…' She hated that she was so weak, so lily-livered with him—hated how her body screamed for him. And yet somehow she revelled in it, revelled in the new dimension he had brought to her existence.

'And it is better than fighting…' He was kissing her neck, kissing it so deeply surely he was bruising her, and bruising her mind as well… His voice was a plea as he tried so hard just to talk to her. 'Millie, I can't do *that* without this…'

He carried her to the water's edge and laid her down. It had been pointless her wearing a bikini top, because it was now halfway around her neck. Then it was completely tossed aside, and Millie watched with a fleeting smile as the ocean claimed an hour of shopping.

She could feel the wet sand on her back as her body curved in—could feel the cool weightlessness of the water contrasting with his warm, heavy body as he lay on top of her. Hands that had once been tentative were brave now as she slid his bathers down, her nails dragging into his firm buttocks as the ocean claimed its second gift. She savoured the taste of the salt water on his skin as his shoulders enveloped her, one strong arm lifting her head above the water as his other hand wrestled with the flimsy straps of her bikini bottom. His erection was stronger than the ocean as it pressed against her—his need, his want for her all-encompassing, as hers was for him.

The blissful stab as he entered her, swelling deep within, made her whole body arch into his. He rocked deep within her, defying the waves, each rush of water up her body a contrast as he pulled his gift back. Every time she attempted to catch her breath as the pounding waves receded he filled her further, refusing her even a second to regroup. Her calves locked behind him as Levander surged inside her, where he had lived in her restless, aching dreams every night since first they'd been together. With each deep thrust she welcomed him back, and as measured as the ocean an orgasm so intensely fierce she felt as if she was going under claimed her again.

When his first ever playtime was over, when they were too tired to be brittle, too happily exhausted to argue as blazing day faded into a long, long night he told her.

Some.

Drip-fed her his torture—about the lying-down rooms they'd been sent to, about the staff. Though most of them had cared, quite simply there hadn't been enough of anything to go around.

Not enough food, or clothes or nappies—the most basic necessities all lacking—and attention, affection, the most thinly stretched of them all.

Before he revealed anything though, he made it absolutely clear that he never wanted her sympathy or pity—but that if somehow, by knowing him, she could maybe understand him, maybe choose to stay, if that was what it took, then he would tell her.

'She was his cleaner.' Staring up at the sky as they lay together, wrapped in each other's arms, he told her, walked her slowly through his very private hell.

'When she fell pregnant…well, I am told my father said he would keep her as his mistress, that he would provide for her and the baby. But that was not enough for my mother. She wanted him to marry her, or at least be faithful… On both counts he refused. She was very proud, very headstrong….'

Millie smiled as he stated the obvious.

'What?'

'I like her already—you're clearly your mother's son.'

He frowned as if it had never entered his head—frowned and then smiled as he shrugged, as he accepted a little piece of his history. 'To her family's fury, she walked out on him.'

'Her family's fury?'

'Her family disowned her—and that was okay. For more than three years we were okay. Until…' He wasn't smiling now, took a moment to regroup, to continue. 'My father got married to Nina. She was pregnant with the twins, and my mother guessed that my father and Nina were planning to flee. He gave her a lot of money all of a sudden, and came round many nights in a row to play with me—but those are the sort of plans that can't be discussed. She had a cough then. I can remember that. But he didn't know how ill she was. All of a sudden my father wasn't there any more, and my mother was really ill. When she left me at the baby house to go to the hospital she said my father would come.'

'And they didn't trace him…'

He gave a wry laugh, but it wasn't mocking. 'They were not even married. She registered me with his surname, and in Russia you take you father's first name as your middle—Levander Ivanovich Kolovsky, which means Levander son of Ivan—but who was going to search? I was just one of many. Better than most, really.'

'How?'

'Because I had her for a little while… ' He closed his eyes and she didn't know if he was blocking it out or seeing it again. 'I had once seen normal—I knew how to behave, knew how to read, to write, because she had taught me. Without that I know I would have gone crazy.'

'Like the child you told me about—the one who screamed at bedtime?'

'Like him.' Levander nodded. 'But I am stronger because I had her. That is not me being sentimental—' he checked that she understood '—already I knew normal—we were poor, but we were happy.'

'You can really remember?'

'Very well.' He nodded again. 'I had a lot of time to look back. I remember her reading, I remember her singing, I remember I swore and she slapped me…' He actually laughed at the memory. 'Most of the children there don't even have that. They are abandoned there at birth—that is all they know. I did not scream or cry—I believed my father was one day going to come and get me, because that was the last thing she told me. I kept to myself when I could, and learned to defend myself when I couldn't—and I studied hard. I achieved the Gold Medal at school, which goes to the best student. I was accepted at Moscow University, and then my father found me.'

'He'd been looking?'

'Apparently he sent money every month—and letters and cards, but I never saw them. I don't know if my mother's family kept the money. I just don't know. Eventually he traced me. It caused a lot of problems when I came to Australia. Iosef and Aleksi were furious with my father. Furious that he had left me behind and that they had never been told. They tried hard to get close to me, but I just couldn't trust them. I was not easy to live with. I was so angry with them—with the world.'

'And now?'

'Iosef left to study medicine as soon as he was old enough. Aleksi is in London. We have never been close. I never let them get close…' he finally admitted.

'What about Annika?'

'Annika…' He shook his head hopelessly. 'She just wants everything to be fine.'

'Can it ever be?'

'I don't know. This is the first time I have ever spoken about it….' She thought about her own fears, her own doubts, her own worries, and tried to fathom never once voicing them.

'They are so ashamed of the past…but it is *my* past, Millie. If they cannot accept that then they can never accept me. The finest tailor, the cars, the money—they only dress up the outside. That was my life, and they cannot face it. To this day my father and Nina live in fear that the secret will get out—that people will judge them…'

And it would be so easy to judge, Millie thought. So easy to loathe a man who could walk away from his own son.

'He says that he regrets—' His voice broke, just a tiny husk in that strong fluid voice, and it ripped through her. 'He regrets what I have suffered, and now he is trying to make it up to me.'

'Can he?'

'I don't know.'

She was crying as he answered, and trying so hard not to show it—scared to wipe the tears away in case he saw them. She could see now just how much Janey's words would have eaten at him—that his own child might have existed unknown on the other side of the world…

'All that time—all my life there—I wanted him to come and get me. I wanted him to see me and be proud—and in the end, yes, he did come and get me. I got my wish.'

But it was so very little, and so very late.

'Can you?' Millie rasped. 'Can you somehow forgive him?'

'That is something I need to decide.' Levander nodded at the insurmountable challenge. 'And given his health, I'd better make my decision soon.'

Levander's next question pierced the long silence that followed. 'Would marriage be so bad? Do you see now how important it is to me?'

'It won't keep us together…' She swallowed hard, wondered how she could ask from him what she needed to hear. 'Levander, if you don't love me…a piece of paper isn't going to change anything.'

'It will change a lot for me.'

Which wasn't the answer she wanted. Even if he was trying to help, with each word he just hurt her more.

'I would look after you; I would never be unfaithful; I would always do the right thing by you. And if you still have doubts, then I tell you this—we don't have to love each other for this to work. We will love our child, and that will be enough.'

CHAPTER ELEVEN

'THE MALDIVES, perhaps…?' Katina suggested, handing Levander a thick brochure.

He gave it barely a glance, glancing down at his watch and clearly itching to get back to work. 'Any preference, Millie?'

'I don't know…' Millie mumbled, hating that they were back. Her suntan was fading only marginally more slowly than her hopes for the future she had been so full of on the island—hopes that had convinced her to say yes to the wedding.

Back in the real world—back where clocks ticked and people demanded and schedules dictated—she wasn't quite so sure they could make it. Wasn't quite so sure that a baby, that sex, was going to be enough to see them through.

'We'll have to go to London and see my family— they'll want to meet you.'

'They will meet me at the wedding,' Levander answered easily. But, seeing her worried face, he gave a little frown. 'There is no problem—I will pay for them to come out, absolutely.'

'It's not the money,' Millie said, blushing as Katina coolly listened on. 'They won't be able to come to Australia even if they could afford it. Austin could never go on a plane—it would be too distressing for him. Mum and Dad have enough trouble getting him into a car—he hates anything like that.'

'Who's Austin?' Katina asked pen poised.

'Millie's brother.'

'And he doesn't like to travel?'

God, she hated this—hated having to explain herself to strangers. Hated that they'd been back in Melbourne only a few days and they were already in their second meeting.

A meeting to arrange their wedding.

Somehow, the fact that he could never love her had made her decision easier.

No more pretending that in time love might grow. No more kidding herself that he wanted her for any other reason than the baby they had made.

And even if her heart said she was marrying for all the wrong reasons, on the flipside it told her she was marrying for the right ones.

She loved Levander—loved him enough to give him the security he craved for his child.

Loved their baby enough to give it one home.

'Would you prefer we marry in London?' Levander offered. Katina's lips pursed, but Millie shook her head, thinking of the pressure on her family, the nightmare of her mum attempting to socialise with the Kolovskys.

'I think here might be better.'

'Then we will marry here and go to London for the honeymoon,' Levander suggested. And even though it made perfect sense—even though he had offered her the choice—not for the first time she felt railroaded, as if the Kolovskys had got their way once again.

'I just don't see why it has to be so soon,' Millie attempted again.

'It is not so soon,' Levander said dismissively. 'In Russia, a marriage normally happens quickly—between one and three months after the engagement is announced. And given you are already five months pregnant…surely it is better we marry quickly? Get it over with…'

He made it sound like a trip to the dentist.

'The Kolovskys calendar is full for the next thee months,' Katina explained, a little less patiently than she had the last ten times. 'And anyway, if we leave it much longer you're going to have rather a job getting into the dress.'

Another thing she hadn't thought about.

'Do you have any brochures? I don't know…' She gave a helpless shrug. 'So I can get an idea of what I want…'

'*An idea of what you want?*' Katina stared at her in bemusement.

'For my dress.'

'Millie—you're marrying Levander. Did you really think we'd be sending you down to the local bridal shop? Your dress is already taken care off. Nina herself is going to come and do the final fittings. Right.' Shuffling her notes, Katina stood up. 'Have a think about your honeymoon and let me know tomorrow…'

'Final fittings?' Millie turned on Levander the second they were alone. 'I wasn't wrong that night—I actually thought I was being ridiculous, but my dress *is* already chosen—already hanging there half made, waiting for a bride to step into it.'

'Of course.' Levander looked at her as if she were completely mad. 'There are probably fifty gowns there—and you will get the best one, naturally. Now, if that is all, then I should get back to work.'

Even though her mind was abuzz with wedding preparations, and her nights were filled with Levander, as the days slipped by more and more Millie realised her idea of a family and Levander's were poles apart.

The tenderness they had found on the island seemed to have evaporated as soon as they'd touched down on the mainland. The only trace of it to be found was in the nights, when he reached for her, but it only disintegrated again every morning.

And for Millie the disquiet grew.

The uneasy homesickness that washed in at times positively overwhelmed her each and every time she rang her family to update them on the rapidly approaching wedding day. Hearing her mother's genuine wonder and delight as she asked about the baby's progress was such a contrast to Nina's coldness that it was almost more than Millie could bear.

'I'm having the teeniest panic attack.' On the eve of her wedding, Anton was in his element when Millie dropped by, humming the 'Wedding March' as Millie paced on. 'And I want you to be completely honest with me. Would it be a terrible *faux pas* to wear Kolovsky to a Kolovsky wedding?'

She had to laugh. 'You're asking *me* for fashion advice?'

'I know.' He clapped his hands to his cheeks. 'Oooh, thank you, thank you, thank you, for asking me to give you away—it's going to be the happiest day of my life.'

At least it would be for one of them, Millie thought, bursting into tears for the forty-second time that day.

'It's nerves,' Anton assured her.

'It is,' Millie sniffed. She badly wanted to talk, to tell someone her tumble of thoughts, but after Janey it was just too big, too scary to indulge in something as simple as a much-needed talk between friends. But as she went to grab her bag, as she thought of going back to the hotel to have Nina sticking pins in her for the final check that her dress was perfect, Millie baulked. 'I don't know if I can do this, Anton.'

'It's definitely nerves, honey,' Anton insisted, pulling out a vast hanky and trying to make her smile as she wiped her eyes. 'You know you're the most hated woman in Australia at the moment!'

His weak attempt at humour didn't work.

'I want my mum!'

'Oh, you poor baby…'

He led her to the back of the gallery, where he made her a big mug of hot chocolate with marshmallows. It was the kindest thing anyone had done for her since she'd landed there—the kindest thing anyone had done for her without wanting something in return.

'I know it must kill you not to have your family here, but you do have friends. I was at the airport when you arrived back, you know…' He smiled at her shocked expression. 'You know I never sleep—I popped out to get the paper and there was that filth sprawled all over it. I figured you could use some moral support—not that I even got close... Talk to me, Millie.'

'I can't.'

'I know after Janey you're afraid to trust anyone,' he said gently, and as she opened her mouth to argue he spoke over her. 'But I *am* on your side. I'll come over tonight the second I lock up, and I won't leave your side till the wedding...' He gave a tiny wince. 'I've just got to pop to the hairdresser's at midday.'

'I'm sure there'll be one in my room you can use,' Millie said with a wry smile, but Anton shook his head.

'Luigi would never forgive me. I'm going to hold your hand every step of the way. Once the wedding's over, once everything's calmed down, things will be so much easier...'

'I hope so.'

'I guess the question is—do you love him?' He didn't follow it up with anything silly—just asked her the one thing in all this she could answer honestly.

'Of course.'

'Well, that's all right, then.'

'How is your mother?' Levander asked, sitting on the bedroom chair and smothering a yawn.

'Teary,' Millie admitted, standing in her dress as Nina and Sophia, the dressmaker, tugged none too gently. She hated how clinical it all was—hated that a silly little thing like him seeing her in dress before the big day mattered to her so. 'Wishing she could be here.'

'You'll see her very soon.'

'I know.' Millie stared fixedly ahead wishing it was two o'clock tomorrow and it was all over with.

'I have to go soon…' Levander glanced at his watch

'Fine.'

'Iosef's plane is due in—I'd like to be there to meet him. We are going out for dinner with my father.'

'Of course.'

'Perfect.' Nina stood back and admired her top dressmaker's handiwork—as well she might. A sheath of thick ivory Kolovsky silk had been sculpted to Millie's body, every stitch, every nip, somehow turning her into the beautiful bride she had to be. 'Sophia will be over tomorrow to help with any last-minute alterations. Now, no eating from now till after the wedding.' Nina frowned, running a very unwelcome hand over Millie's slight bump. 'I can get you some of the special herbal tea the models use—to get a bit of fluid off.'

Millie didn't even deign to respond—just peeled off the dress and stood silent as Nina flounced out of the bedroom, carrying the dress as if it were some precious child.

'Ignore her,' Levander said.

'Oh, I assure you I try.'

'I know it is hard—to marry without your family. But it is not as if…' He didn't finish, so Millie did it for him.

'It's not as if it's a real wedding.'

'Of course it is real,' Levander countered, but Millie shook her head.

'You know, this should be like a dream come true— a fabulous wedding, A-list guests, a designer dress, a baby on the way, the man—' She stopped herself. How she wanted to tell him how she felt—that she loved him so much it hurt. Even if she understood that they were marrying for the sake of the child they had created it was killing her inside to know that was the only reason. That if it wasn't for their baby Levander Kolovsky would never have considered her as his bride. 'I guess it's true—we should be more careful what we wish for.'

'I don't understand.'

'It's a saying—be careful what you wish for, it might come true.'

As she delivered the saying the confusion that had been etched on his face disappeared. All expression did. Always pale, his skin was now as white as marble; even those beautiful lips were dusky in his grey features.

'That is how you feel?'

His voice seemed to be coming from far away, and his question confused her. Because she did know how she felt. Millie knew as she stood there before him that she loved him, and that was what was killing her. Being close to him and knowing she couldn't really have him— that this distant, remote, yet at times incredibly emotive man, couldn't give her the piece of him that she needed.

'You feel trapped?' Levander pushed.

And she nodded—because trapped *was* how she felt. Not by the situation, but by her feelings. She realised then that, as impressive as Levander's reasons were for a hasty marriage, if she didn't love him, didn't want him with every fibre of her being, she'd have walked away— would have made it on her own.

Would have managed just fine.

'Come!' Waltzing back into the bedroom and not

even knocking, Nina called to Levander. 'We need to get to the airport, and Millie should get a good night's sleep.' Over her shoulder, unwittingly for once, Nina hurled another knife. 'Enjoy your last night of freedom!'

CHAPTER TWELVE

ANTON, for all that he wasn't family, made a very good mother of the bride—spoiling her rotten, policing everyone. And there were plenty to police. The hairdresser, the manicurist, the dressmaker, the make-up artists…

Artists!

Millie needed two, apparently. One for her face and the other to concentrate solely on her décolletage—to even out her fading tan and ensure her cleavage was spectacularly arranged.

Anton even made a fuss of Annika, Millie's very stunning bridesmaid and half-sister-in-law to be—who, given Millie was about to share her surname, actually opened up a touch as the room buzzed with the frenzy of getting her ready.

Finally, when Anton had shooed everyone out and it was just the three of them, he gave Millie the biggest of smiles, then promptly burst into tears. 'You look ravishing.'

'Thank you.'

'Now, I'm going to race over to Luigi's and get just

a smidgen of product put through my hair—and you, honey…'

'I know.' Millie shivered at the prospect of ringing her parents. 'Maybe I should ring them after the wedding…'

'No.' Anton was insistent. 'They'll want to wish you luck. You know you have to do this—by the time you're done I'll be back. Look after her, Annika,' Anton called, flying out of the door.

'Maybe it would be better to wait?' Annika gave a sympathetic smile and said absolutely the wrong thing. 'You might ruin your make-up.'

She didn't want this.

Tears were filling her exquisitely made-up eyes and she blinked them back, staring at her reflection and trying, for the thousandth time, to tell herself that everything was okay.

She was marrying the man she loved.

Marrying the father of her child.

Standing in her stunning wedding dress, with a packed church waiting to share in this most special moment.

So why did it feel as if she were walking to the gallows?

It was just homesickness, Millie told herself. If only her family could be here… But that didn't fit—because, as much as she missed them, it wasn't actually her family she needed today…

It was Levander…

Or rather his love.

Fiddling with the huge diamond on her ring finger, she recalled their lovemaking, tried to hone in on the magic they shared. But no matter how much she tried, how much she wanted to convince herself, at the end of the day it was the baby they were marrying for…

But was it enough?

'Your family must be very proud,' Annika attempted as Millie tried to hold down the single glass of water she'd managed that morning. 'Believe it or not, my father is proud too.'

'Believe it or not?' Millie frowned. 'Why wouldn't he be proud of Levander?'

'He is proud of Levander. I was talking about…well you two…' Annika was still going on, frowning at Millie's pale reflection and without invitation adding another dash of blusher. 'Even though you're not perhaps who we'd have first chosen it has all worked out well—Papa has got his wish and more.'

'His wish?'

'Last night it was made official,' she prattled on, less reserved without her mother around. 'My father always said that the Kolovsky empire would go to the first of his children who gave him a grandchild. And we all knew that he wanted that person to be Levander—the son he would give anything to make happy. Levander has been a driving force in the company and Papa is desperate for him to stay on. That night when you two met, when I was pleading with Levander to grant father his wish, he was so adamant the answer was no….' She smiled down to Millie's stomach. 'Who knows how Levander's mind works?'

Not she. Millie's hands went to her stomach, held the tiny life that might not have been such an accident after all, and wondered if Levander, in his own dark way, had somehow decided to claim what he thought he deserved.

'Maybe he will get to see his grandchild too…' Annika said, her eyes following Millie's hands. 'You should have a scan.'

'I've had one.'

'Find out this time…' Annika stood back to admire her handiwork, to check that the bride they all so desperately wanted was passable enough—was good enough to take the family name. Millie felt like slapping her. 'Let's just hope we can tell Papa he is getting a grandson…'

Annika's mobile rang she turned her back. 'Hold on a moment… Levander—what does he want?'

To make his father happy.

The biggest most difficult, most terrifying decision of her life was suddenly made incredibly simple.

She could almost have accepted him marrying her for the baby—marrying her out of duty—but the thought that he had engineered the situation in order to please his father, or worse to inherit the Kolovsky empire, filled her with horror.

Maybe she was an old-fashioned girl after all, Millie decided. Because the only thing she could marry for was love.

'I'll just be a moment…' Annika gave Millie a worried smile. "Everything is okay—you just keep on getting ready.'

As Annika fled to the bedroom Millie could hear her shouting, hear yet another Kolovsky argument breaking out, but she didn't even notice. The second the bedroom door closed, Millie pulled off her headdress, yanked the beastly dress down and pulled on her jeans, slipping on some runners and grabbing her purse.

As Levander had said, it wasn't a prison… All she had to do was open the doors and press the lift button, then walk calmly out through the hotel foyer. Every waiting camera was on the lookout for a blushing bride in white, not a pale woman in jeans.

Walking along the tree-lined street, she didn't look back—not once. She just willed herself to be calm, to keep on walking, until she hit the main road—and boarded a tram that clattered past, not knowing where it was taking her and not really caring.

'End of the line, love.'

She hadn't even noticed the tram had come to a stop, her mind lost in a whir of thoughts—trying and failing to picture Levander's face when he found out his bride wasn't coming, Anton's hysterics when he got back to the hotel to find her gone, the shock of the guests, the blitz of headlines, her parents' reaction…

Maybe she *should* have just gone through with it, Millie begged of herself as she stepped off the tram and stood shivering on the street. The bright winter sun that had held so much promise this morning was now shrouded in grey, and a bitter wind was skimming the Tasman and blowing across the bay.

St Kilda.

Where their rollercoaster ride had started—the last stop on their first date, on that magical tour of Melbourne. But somehow the world was a greyer, bleaker place without Levander beside her.

As she headed into the café, where they had sat and talked for hours, it was as if a curtain had lifted and the scenery had been changed. Happy families were at every table: children plunging long spoons into deep glasses of ice-cream, young, beautiful couples wading through the papers and idly watching the world go by, unaware of the seamier clientele that would frequent it later.

Sitting at a corner booth, Millie ordered coffee, clasped her hands around the vast mug and wondered if she'd ever be warm again—wondered how she could go back and face them all.

And she'd have to.

Her passport, her clothes…

Oh, God, what had she done? Maybe she should have just gone through with it. Certainly she should have spoken to Levander. But how—*how* could she…?

How could she tell him that the autonomous, principled man she'd fallen in love with didn't match up to a man who would make a baby to appease his father—however high the stakes?

'I am sorry.' His rich, deep voice broke into her racing thoughts, and her eyes darted up to where he stood over her. 'May I sit?'

She couldn't speak, so instead she nodded, bracing herself for a vitriolic outburst Levander style. She was bemused at the hesitancy in him, stunned when he took her mug of coffee from her and held her hands, before taking a deep breath and finally talking.

'I am sorry—sorry to shame you. But it is not your shame, it is mine—remember that. I will tell everyone.'

'Sorry?' Millie frowned. His apology completely unexpected, and she was unable to look at him—just stared
at his fingers entwined around hers, utterly perplexed by
what he was saying and flailing for a response. 'It isn't
about shame, Levander. It's... I just couldn't do it.
Couldn't marry you knowing—'

'Pardon?' He interrupted her stumbling explanation—and for the first time she managed to look at him,
saw the confusion in his eyes that mirrored her own.

'I didn't mean to run away—I wasn't planning it. I
just...'

'You jilted me?' She winced at the phrase, but the
question in his voice made no sense—and what made
even less sense was the tiny flicker of a smile playing
on the edge of his lips. '*You* jilted *me?*'

'Why do you think I'm here?' She glanced to the
large clock on the wall, and then back to him. 'Why,
when we should be walking out of the church arm in
arm around now, am I sitting in a café in St Kilda,
bawling my eyes out?'

'Because *I* jilted *you.*' His shocking words halted
her. 'Because half an hour before you were due to leave
for the church I rang Annika and told her I couldn't do
it to you—couldn't force you to be my wife...'

'You jilted me?' It was so appalling, so embarrass-
ing, she could barely get her head around it. 'I was left
at the altar...?'

'Ah...' Levander shook his head. 'Apparently you
were never going to make it to the altar...'

And she realised then why he'd given that strange
smile when she'd made her stumbling explanation. The

humiliation she'd thought she'd inflicted on him, the embarrassment, the shame she'd thought she'd wreaked on another human being, eradicated now. Millie actually managed a shocked giggle as she remembered Annika shouting on the phone as she'd sped out of the room.

'Can I ask why?' Her smile faded as he confronted her, the real issues bobbing back up to the dark surface. 'Why you chose not to marry me—why you think you and our child would be better off without me?'

'I don't,' Millie sobbed. 'I won't… It's just… Annika told me about your father—that she had begged you to have a child the night we met.'

'My whole family has begged me to procreate for years now.' Levander shrugged. 'Why does that shock you? You heard us talking that night…'

'I didn't hear *that,*' Millie gasped.

'Millie, I am loath to give him even a few more years' work from me—do you really think for one minute I would sign away my life for him?'

'I don't know,' Millie admitted. She was crying now—crying in a way she only had since she'd met him. From the day she'd left his arms and headed back to England, from when the pregnancy test had proved positive, since he'd invaded her world and stripped her bare, inflamed her raw emotions till everything was in Technicolor—every thought, every feeling, more intense somehow. 'I don't know if I was just looking for an excuse not to marry you…'

'Would you believe that I am not trying to appease my father if I tell you that last night I spoke with him? We went out, and he offered me—'

'I know about that.' Millie shivered. 'I know that the first child to produce a Kolovsky heir gets the prize…'

'I declined. It is a ridiculous idea. How could I solely inherit when I have two brothers and a sister?' He took in her shocked reaction. 'I told him that I would continue to work for him—but only if I can do it from London.'

'London?' Millie blinked at him. 'You were prepared to move to London?'

'I still am.' He stated it as if it was obvious. 'I was hoping when I said it that we would be doing it together, as a proper family, but now I accept that is not possible. However, I still want to be the best father I can be—and I cannot do that from Australia. Even if we are not together, I know you will treat me fairly.' He looked at her stunned face and explained a touch further. 'I trust you, Millie.'

And for someone with his past, Millie realised that trust was almost better than love. Not that it helped right now—not that it helped when the man of your dreams was telling you the reason that he couldn't actually bring himself to marry you. But later it would. Millie knew that later, when she replayed this conversation, somehow the fact that after all he'd been through he actually trusted her might be just enough sustain her in the end.

'I woke up this morning and I realised I trust you—that marriage is not needed for the sake of our child. I know that you will put our baby's interests first—that I do not have to force myself into the picture to be there.'

'Because you *are* there.' Millie trembled. 'Whether we're married or not, friends or not, you will always be this child's father. Always.'

'I know that now. I know you would never keep me from my child. Not like—' He stopped himself then, and even though she was drowning in her own grief, choking on her own feelings, something in his voice reached her.

Her forehead creased into a frown. 'Levander—things were different then. It wasn't like now, when you can pop on a plane—they thought you were safe, they thought…' Her voice petered out as she looked beyond his effortless beauty, beyond those brooding eyes, and right into his very soul. She saw not pain, not bitterness or regret, but raw, unbridled agony.

The dawning suspicion, when it came to her, was so utterly devastating that her first reaction was to recoil, to close her eyes and block out what she could see written in his eyes.

'He knew, didn't he?'

'No.' Levander closed his eyes, pulled back his hand. But Millie wasn't about to let go, grabbing it back and holding tightly. 'He didn't know anything.'

'She did, though…' Millie whispered. 'Nina knew, didn't she?'

'Don't go there—it is not worth the pain.'

'Whose pain?' Millie asked angrily, protectively. 'What about *your* pain?'

'If my family were to know—if my father ever found out what she did… Annika, Iosef…' He dragged in a breath. 'They cannot know—it would finish him.'

'It won't finish me.' Somehow her voice was firm. 'You said you trust me.'

'I do.'

'So tell me.'

He swallowed so hard it was if he was choking. 'What I told you before—all of it is true except…' His eyes found hers then, his hands held hers, gripping them tightly as he told her the truth—the real truth this time. Not the Kolovsky version, but the truth of a little boy who had seen far, far too much. 'The day before I went to the baby house we went to my father's—Nina answered; she was pregnant. I remember that, and I remember my father wasn't home. My mother told Nina how sick she was. I remember because it was the first time I realised that my mother was actually dying—she was coughing and crying, and she told Nina her family could not afford to have me when she was gone…' He faltered for a moment, so Millie held his hand tighter.

She preferred the old version. Life had somehow been easier when she'd thought him bitter and jealous. The appalling truth was more than anyone should have to bear.

'Nina didn't care. I just remember them arguing. My mother was crying so hard she could barely breathe, and then Nina shooed us away as if we were gypsies come begging.'

Some agonies were just too big for tears. Life was so unbearable at times that to break down and merely cry would almost be an insult. Millie wanted to howl—wanted to scream at a world that had been so cruel. Rage was churning in her—a rage so strong it almost propelled her from her seat, to find Nina, to tell Ivan… But somehow she held it in check—she knew it couldn't possibly help him.

'Does *she* know…' She tried to keep the hatred from her voice. 'Does she know you can remember?'

'The day I found out you were pregnant I told Nina. Now she has to live with her fear. We all have to live with our mistakes. Last night you said you should be careful what you wish for…' A mirthless smile ghosted his lips, and his English was less than perfect as he struggled to tell her more about his past. 'When my mother took me to *dom rebyonka,* the baby house, she told me it would not be for long—that I was to be good and wait, and that my father would come and get me. I don't know if she went back to speak with him again. I don't really want to know. But every night I looked out of the window and I wished—I wished for him, for a family, and later as I got older I wished too for money, and I wished for beautiful women. I got every last wish. Compared to those poor bastards still there, I have nothing to complain about.'

'Oh, but you do.'

She got it then—as much as anyone who hadn't lived his life possibly could. Since she'd found out she was pregnant she'd wondered if she was up to being a mother—the mother she wanted to be—if she could provide for her child the happy, secure childhood her own parents had given her. But for Levander there were no happy memories, no foundations on which to build. Just a much too late glimpse of family was all he had known. A family fractured by his very presence. His arrival had split the family, caused his half-brothers' anger and blame, his father's guilt, his stepmother's fear.

'I wanted us to be married. I thought that maybe then I would have more rights—I knew that if the courts had to choose between us, if my past came out…'

'There'll be no court,' Millie whispered. 'I told you there was never going to be court—and anyway, Levander, no court would hold this against you. None of this is your fault.'

'I know that now.' Levander nodded, and with tears swimming in her eyes she tried to look at him as she attempted to say the bravest words of her life—to tell the man who had just jilted her, the man who had wanted marriage for all the wrong reasons, that no matter how others in his life had treated him, she loved him—loved him for everything he was.

'That night was the most rash, reckless thing I've ever done—but it wasn't an accident. I didn't fall into bed with you that night because of your looks or your money or…' Staring skywards for clarity was her worst mistake. Tears tumbled down her cheeks as she rewound a touch—aimed for total honesty. 'Okay, maybe your looks *did* play a part—but they weren't enough to hold me. It was *you*, Levander—you were the first person I'd trusted, the first person I gave myself to. And whatever the outcome—that night wasn't an accident. As dazzled as they were, my eyes were open. Did it never enter your head that all this time I've loved you?'

But how could it have? Millie realised as he frowned over at her. How could a man like Levander, who had never known it, believe in something as simple and as complicated as love?

'The *only* reason I couldn't go through with our marriage in the end was because I knew you'd never love me.'

'You *love* me?' He practically barked the question. 'Through-all-of-this-you-say-that-you-have-loved-me?'

'I'm afraid so.'

'How?' His question actually eked out a half-laugh. 'How could you love me when I was so horrible to you?'

'I just did…' Millie sobbed. 'I just do.'

'Tell me what this love is,' Levander asked. 'Tell me what love feels like.'

'Awful.' A new batch of tears was coming, and she covered her face with her hands, wishing he wouldn't torture her so. Surely knowing was enough?

'But it is good at times?'

'Lots of times.'

'So when you love someone, you think about them all the time?'

'All the time.' Millie nodded glumly.

'Like you think you are going crazy?' Levander checked.

'Completely crazy.'

'Would love make you worry that you are too bitter, too cynical? That somehow you might taint the other…?'

Peeking at his face from behind her fingers, Millie felt the world stop as Levander continued.

'And because of this love, do you want only what's best for the other person?'

'Always,' Millie breathed, and he took her hands down from her face and held them as he spoke on softly.

'This love would make you spend far too much on a picture because you *have* to have it—you have to have something…'

'Tangible?' Millie offered, only he didn't understand.

'Something you can feel and see and touch to know that it is real.'

'Tangible.' Levander nodded, as if he really liked the word. 'You buy an expensive picture because it is tangible.'

'Sort of.' She gulped, crying and laughing and loving him for faltering over a single world.

'So if you love someone—even though you want to spend every minute with them, even though all you want to do is be with them—still, if that is where you think they do not want to be, you would let them go? When you see her standing beautiful in her wedding dress, but her eyes are resigned…'

She wasn't laughing now. This was an insight he was giving her—insight into how lonely, how unsure of his own worth he was, of the terrible effects of growing up in a world utterly devoid of love.

Levander hadn't been able to tell her he loved her because he didn't even know what it was.

'Are you telling me you love me, Levander?' Millie whispered.

'I'm just checking with myself first,' he said.

From anyone else the pause that followed would have been an insult, but from Levander it was anything but—just a delicious, wondrous wait as he processed his thoughts, as he assimilated all the feelings he'd never till now experienced.

'I-love-you.' He said it like that, each word a firm statement, and even if they were the three little words she'd wanted so badly to hear, when he said them—when he looked at her and actually said them—nothing could have prepared her for the impact of him saying them.

If she lived past a hundred, Millie swore there and then that every time he graced her with those words she would relive this moment. Even though he hadn't even known what it meant to receive love, somehow he had found the courage to love her.

'I love you,' he said again, and hearing the honesty, the wonder in his voice as he joined up the puzzle, knowing how alien it was to him, made the words all the more precious to her.

'Why are we sitting here, then?' Millie smiled through her tears. 'Why don't we go...?' She'd been about to say home, but Levander's hotel room had never been that, to either of them. But as her voice trailed off, Levander filled in for her.

'There's a church decorated and waiting, the priest is booked, and we've got a licence...'

'Everyone will have gone.'

'Perfect!'

'But I'm in jeans....' Millie gave a shocked laugh

'Even better.' Leaning over, he kissed her—one tiny kiss, but it was so laced with love, so utterly chaste and tender, it confirmed utterly what he'd just told her.

He loved her—*that* was enough—for anything.

'I will ring the church...' As Levander turned on his phone he rolled his eyes. 'Fifty missed calls—can you imagine Nina's face?' He winced as it rang loudly. 'It's Iosef. I won't take it. He will understand...'

'We need witnesses,' Millie said gently, as the ringing died away. 'Two, I believe. Why don't you ask your brothers?'

'My *half*...' Levander started but didn't finish. Love

was flooding in now, and shining its light on so many dark places.

'Doesn't one have to be a female?' Mille asked, but Levander waved her away.

'Between the two of them—I'm sure they can rustle one up.'

And she watched, smiling, as he took the call—watched as he laughed with his brother as they shared their first secret, arranged for him and Aleksi to slip away from the drama unfolding back at the Kolovsky house and pick them up to take them to the church.

'What did he say?'

'That he would be proud to be there—and I hope you don't mind, but we have another guest…' As her face literally paled, Levander just laughed. 'Anton—he's distraught. They are on their way.' Standing up, he took her hand, led her out onto the street and into her new life. 'Now—may I suggest that we go and get married.'

EPILOGUE

THE only advantage to Levander's past was that he loved shopping.

And there was plenty to be done.

A vast, sprawling home on the outskirts of London had to be furnished and decorated and filled with memories and babies and love.

'I can see why she did it.'

They were lying on the grass—Sashar kicking on the rug between them. She watched the sky darken, feeling his hand on her soft stomach. They hadn't even made it indoors yet since Levander had come home from work. Still in his suit, he lay beside her, chatting, yawning, lazy and utterly relaxed, enjoying the evening with their baby.

Sashar Levander Kolovsky.

She'd loved looking through Russian names, and had been completely unable to make a decision. But a couple of days before he was born Millie had stumbled on the name Sashar.

'It means reward, I think,' Levander had told her. 'Or God remembers…'

Both meanings had seemed to fit, and now he was here, lying beside them—the absolute image of his father.

And his father's father.

Sometimes Millie felt a stab of guilt—guilt that they were on the other side of the world when his father was so sick, that maybe if they'd stayed somehow bridges could have been built.

But somehow by leaving they had been. Sashar had brought them the most surprising gift of all—forgiveness, where Millie had thought there could never be.

'I can see Nina felt she had no choice...'

Sometimes he spoke about it. Not often, but sometimes—just little snatches of stolen childhood—and she never cried on the outside. Just wept on the inside for all he'd seen and all that he'd never had.

'She had to think of her unborn children. If she had told my father—if he had insisted they take me to Australia too—well, they may never have got there.' He stared down at Sashar. 'I think I understand now.'

'And your father?' Millie gulped, wishing she could understand too—could be as big as Levander and somehow find it in her to forgive.

'He told me when I turned down his offer that I was like my mother—too strong willed and stubborn for my own good. But he was smiling when he said it. I guess he banked on how tough she was—convinced himself we would be okay. He couldn't have known that I was in an orphanage, waiting for him to come. You know, a family would come sometimes—dressed in beautiful clothes, smelling of rich perfume. They would bring chocolate, or gifts. I never got one—too old, too angry looking, too much trouble…'

'They didn't give you a gift?'

'The gift was for the child they would take—they were there to choose the child that would join their family. I wished that someone would choose me. Still, I got my wish in the end—you came back for me.'

He bent over and kissed her, and this time she did cry. Because, yes, he'd got his wish in the end, but it had been way, way too long in the coming. She cried not just for Levander but for all those little children who were too angry, too scared and too much trouble to be loved.

'We could go back…'

'Perhaps.' Levander nodded. 'Soon, I guess. For a holiday. I would like my father to see his grandson.'

'I'm not talking about Australia.' Millie smiled softly, and she felt his body still—so still even his heart seemed to stop for a beat or two.

'I never want to go back. Never again will I set foot in that place. No.' He shook his head, but she could feel his indecision—knew that this wasn't the first time he had considered it.

It wasn't the first time Millie had considered it either.

Seeing him hold his son—cherishing the little life they had created—she had caught the pensive look that dimmed his features now and then, seen the tightening of his jaw as he recalled all he had been through, and had known he was living it again, thinking about all the little ones who weren't as lucky or as loved as Sashar.

'Fine…' Millie nodded, but didn't quite leave it

there. 'If you ever change your mind…if you ever want to talk about it—'

'It isn't like choosing a pet,' Levander insisted.

'It wouldn't be.'

'You don't understand, Millie—the damage that is done. These children are not cute, not easy to love, to live with—'

'I know that, Levander,' Millie broke in. 'My own brother isn't particularly cute or easy to live with. But he is very easy to love and, like my parents, I'd never turn my back on him.'

'No, you never would, would you?' It was a statement, not a question, and his voice faded. He stared down at her, seeing the infinite understanding in her eyes, and knew then that she didn't want easy, that she understood completely what she was saying—knew from her own brother that miracles didn't always happen, was fully aware of all she was prepared to take on.

Knew that he had her for ever.

'Could we do it?'

'One day,' Millie answered softly. 'When we're ready—whenever you're ready…'

And if love could travel, then it surely was travelling now—somewhere a piece of their hearts was already sold to the angriest, least loveable one. A child's wish, sent out to the universe, was in the process of being answered…

MILLS & BOON

MODERN™

On sale 1st February 2008

THE SHEIKH'S VIRGIN PRINCESS
by Sarah Morgan

Karim, Sultan of Zangrar, assumed his bride would be gentle, obedient…but the one he got was far too headstrong for marriage and couldn't be a virgin! But Karim soon discovers she is entirely innocent…

THE VIRGIN'S WEDDING NIGHT
by Sara Craven

Harriet Flint turned to sexy Roan Zandros for a marriage of the utmost convenience… Now he's expecting a wedding night to remember, and is determined to claim his inexperienced bride!

INNOCENT WIFE, BABY OF SHAME
by Melanie Milburne

Patrizio Trelini is convinced his wife Keira has been unfaithful, and throws her out into the cold. Now she's discovered she's pregnant! Will Patrizio believe the baby is his?

THE SICILIAN'S RUTHLESS MARRIAGE REVENGE
by Carole Mortimer

Sicilian billionaire Cesare Gambrelli blames the Ingram dynasty for the death of his beloved sister. The beautiful daughter of the family, Robin, is now the object of his revenge by seduction…

Celebrate 100 years of pure reading pleasure with Mills & Boon®

To mark our centenary, each month we're publishing a special 100th Birthday Edition. These celebratory editions are packed with extra features and include a FREE bonus story.

Now that's worth celebrating!

4th January 2008

The Vanishing Viscountess by Diane Gaston
With FREE story The Mysterious Miss M
This award-winning tale of the Regency Underworld launched Diane Gaston's writing career.

1st February 2008

Cattle Rancher, Secret Son by Margaret Way
With FREE story His Heiress Wife
Margaret Way excels at rugged Outback heroes…

15th February 2008

Raintree: Inferno by Linda Howard
With FREE story Loving Evangeline
A double dose of Linda Howard's heady mix of passion and adventure.

Don't miss out! From February you'll have the chance to enter our fabulous monthly prize draw. See special 100th Birthday Editions for details.

www.millsandboon.co.uk

4 FREE

BOOKS AND A SURPRISE GIFT!

We would like to take this opportunity to thank you for reading this Mills & Boon® book by offering you the chance to take FOUR more specially selected titles from the Modern™ series absolutely FREE! We're also making this offer to introduce you to the benefits of the Mills & Boon® Reader Service™—

- ★ **FREE home delivery**
- ★ **FREE gifts and competitions**
- ★ **FREE monthly Newsletter**
- ★ **Exclusive Reader Service offers**
- ★ **Books available before they're in the shops**

Accepting these FREE books and gift places you under no obligation to buy, you may cancel at any time, even after receiving your free shipment. Simply complete your details below and return the entire page to the address below. You don't even need a stamp!

YES! Please send me 4 free Modern books and a surprise gift. I understand that unless you hear from me. I will receive 6 superb new titles every month for just £2.89 each, postage and packing free. I am under no obligation to purchase any books and may cancel my subscription at any time. The free books and gift will be mine to keep in any case.

P8ZED

Ms/Mrs/Miss/Mr ....Initials ....

BLOCK CAPITALS PLEASE

Surname ....

Address ....

....

....Postcode......................................

Send this whole page to:
UK: FREEPOST CN81, Croydon, CR9 3WZ